ID

PRINCE
OF SCANDAL

PRINCE
OF SCANDAL

BY

ANNIE WEST

MILLS
BOON

First published in Great Britain 2011
by Mills & Boon, an imprint of Harlequin (UK) Limited,
Large Print edition 2011
Eton House, 18-24 Paradise Road,
Richmond, Surrey TW9 1SR

LP

© Annie West 2011

ISBN: 978 0 263 22226 5

Harlequin (UK) policy is to use papers that are natural,
renewable and recyclable products and made from
wood grown in sustainable forests. The logging and
manufacturing process conform to the legal environmental
regulations of the country of origin.

Printed and bound in Great Britain
by CPI Antony Rowe, Chippenham, Wiltshire

For Karen, Reeze and Daisy,
who celebrate with me
and who understand all the rest.
Thank you!

CHAPTER ONE

RAUL stared unseeingly out of the chopper as it followed the coast south from Sydney. He shouldn't be here when the situation at home was so delicately poised. But he had no choice.

What an unholy mess!

His hands bunched into fists and he shifted his long legs restlessly.

The fate of his nation and the well-being of his subjects were at risk. His coronation, his right to inherit the kingdom he'd been born to and devoted his life to, hung in the balance. Even now he could scarcely believe it.

Desperately the lawyers had sought one legal avenue after another but the laws of inheritance couldn't be overturned, not till he became king. And to become king…

The alternative was to walk away and leave his country prey to the rivalries that had grown dangerous under the last king, Raul's father. Civil war had almost ripped the country apart two generations ago. Raul had to keep his people safe from that, no matter what the personal cost.

His people, his need to work for them, had been what kept him going through the bleak wasteland of disillusionment when his world had turned sour years before. When paparazzi had muckraked and insinuated and his dreams had shattered around him, the people of Maritz had stood by him.

He would stand by them now when they most needed him.

Besides, the crown was *his*. Not only by birthright. By dint of every long day, every hour he'd devoted to mastering the myriad royal responsibilities.

He would not renounce his heritage. His destiny.

Tension stiffened every sinew and anger simmered in his blood. Despite a lifetime's dedication to the nation, despite his experience, training and formidable capacity, it had all come down to the decision of a stranger.

It scored his pride that his future, his country's future, depended on this visit.

Raul opened the investigator's report, skimming familiar details.

Luisa Katarin Alexandra Hardwicke. Twenty-four. Single. Self-employed.

He assured himself this would be straightforward. She'd be thrilled and eager. Yet he wished the file contained a photo of this woman who would play such a pivotal role in his life.

He closed the report with a snap.

It didn't matter what she looked like. He wasn't weak like his father. Raul had learned the hard way that beauty could lie. Emotions played a man for a fool. Raul ruled his life, like his kingdom, with his head.

Luisa Hardwicke was the key to safeguarding his kingdom. She could be ugly as sin and it would make no difference.

Damn! The cow shifted, almost knocking Luisa over. Wearily she struggled to regain her footing in the bog at the edge of the creek.

It had been a long, troubling morning with early milking, generator problems and an unexpected call from the bank manager. He'd mentioned a property inspection that sounded ominously like a first step to foreclosure.

She shuddered. They'd fought so long to keep the small farming co-operative going through drought, illness and flood. Surely the bank couldn't shut them down now. Not when they had a chance to turn things around.

Overhead came the rhythmic thunder of a helicopter. The cow shifted uneasily.

'Sightseers?' Sam shouted. 'Or have you been hiding some well-heeled friends?'

'I wish!' The only ones she knew with that much money were the banks. Luisa's stomach coiled in a familiar twist of anxiety. Time was fast running out for the co-op.

Inevitably her mind turned to that other world she'd known so briefly. Where money was no object. Where wealth was taken for granted.

If she'd chosen she could be there now, a rich woman with not a financial worry in the world. If she'd put wealth before love and integrity, and sold her soul in that devil's bargain.

Just the thought of it made her ill.

She'd rather be here in the mud, facing bankruptcy with the people she loved than be as wealthy as Croesus, if it meant giving up her soul.

'Ready, Sam?' Luisa forced herself to focus. She put her shoulder to the cow. 'Now! Slow and steady.'

Finally, between them, they got the animal unstuck and moving in the right direction.

'Great,' Luisa panted. 'Just a little more and—' Her words were obliterated as a whirring helicopter appeared over the rise.

The cow shied, knocking Luisa. She swayed, arms flailing. Then her momentum propelled her forwards into the boggy mess. Wet mud plastered her from face to feet.

'Luisa!' Are you OK?' Her uncle, bless him, sounded more concerned than amused.

She lifted her head and saw the cow, udder swaying, heave onto firm ground and plod away without a backward glance. Gingerly Luisa found purchase in the sodden ground and crawled to her knees, then her feet.

'Perfect.' She wiped slime from her cheeks. 'Mud's supposed to be good for the complexion, isn't it?' She met Sam's rheumy gaze and smiled.

She flicked a dollop of mud away. 'Maybe we should bottle this stuff and try selling it as a skin tonic.'

'Don't laugh, girl. It might come to that.'

Ten minutes later, her overalls, even her face stiff with drying mud, Luisa left Sam and trudged up to her house. Her mind was on this morning's phone call. Their finances looked frighteningly bleak.

She rolled stiff shoulders. At least a shower was only minutes away. A wash, a quick cup of tea and…

She slowed as she topped the hill and saw a helicopter on the grass behind the house. Gleaming metal and glass glinted in the sun. It was high-tech and expensive—a complete contrast to the weathered boards of the house and the ancient leaning shed that barely sheltered the tractor and her rusty old sedan.

Fear settled, a cold hard weight in her stomach. Could this be the inspection the banker had mentioned? So soon?

It took a few moments before logic asserted itself. The bank wouldn't waste money on a helicopter.

A figure appeared from behind the chopper and Luisa stumbled to a halt.

The sun silhouetted a man who was long, lean and elegant. The epitome of urbane masculinity.

She could make out dark hair, a suit that probably cost more than her car and tractor put together, plus a formidable pair of shoulders.

Then he turned and walked a few paces, speaking to someone behind the helicopter. His rangy body moved with an easy grace that bespoke lithe power. A power that belied his suave tailored magnificence.

Luisa's pulse flickered out of rhythm. *Definitely not a banker.* Not with that athletic body.

He was in profile now. High forehead, long aristocratic nose, chiselled mouth and firm chin. Luisa read determination in that solid jaw, and in his decisive gestures. Determination and something completely, defiantly masculine.

Heat snaked through her. Awareness.

Luisa sucked in a startled breath. She'd never before experienced such an instant spark of attraction. Had wondered if she ever would. She couldn't suppress a niggle of disturbing reaction.

Despite his elegant clothes this man looked… dangerous.

Luisa huffed out a choked laugh. Dangerous? He'd probably faint if he got mud on his mirror-polished shoes.

Behind the house, worn jeans, frayed shirts and thick socks flapped on the clothes line. Her mouth twitched. Mr stepped-from-a-glossy-magazine couldn't be more out of place. She forced herself to approach.

Who on earth was he?

He must have sensed movement for he turned.

'Can I help you?' Her voice was husky. She assured herself that had nothing to do with the impact of his dark, enigmatic stare.

'Hello.' His lips tilted in a smile.

She faltered. He was gorgeous. If you were impressed by impossibly handsome in a tough, masculine sort of way. Or gleaming, hooded eyes that intrigued, giving nothing away. Or the tiniest hint of a sexy cleft in his chin.

She swallowed carefully and plastered on a smile.

'Are you lost?' Luisa stopped a few paces away. She had to tilt her chin up to look him in the eye.

'No, not lost.' His crisp deep voice curled with just a hint of an accent. 'I've come to see Ms Hardwicke. I have the right place?'

Luisa frowned, perplexed.

It was a rhetorical question. From his assured tone to his easy stance, as if he owned the farm and she was the interloper, this man radiated confidence. With a nonchalant wave of his hand he stopped the approach of a burly figure rounding the corner of the house. Already his gaze turned back to the homestead, as if expecting someone else.

'You've got the right place.'

She looked from the figure at the rear of the house whose wary stance screamed *bodyguard*, to the chopper where the pilot did an equipment check. Another man in a suit stood talking on a phone. Yet all three were focused on her. Alert.

Who were these people? Why were they here?

A shaft of disquiet pierced her. For the first time ever her home seemed dangerously isolated.

'You have business here?' Her tone sharpened.

Instinct, and the stranger's air of command, as if used to minions scurrying to obey, told her this man was in a league far beyond the local bank manager.

An uneasy sensation, like ice water trickling down her spine, made her stiffen.

'Yes, I need to see Ms Hardwicke.' His eyes flicked to her again then away. 'Do you know where I can find her?'

Something in that single look at her face, not once dropping to her filthy clothes, made her burningly self-conscious. Not just of the mud, but the fact that even clean and in her best outfit she'd feel totally outclassed.

Luisa straightened. 'You've found her.'

This time he really looked. The intensity of that stare warmed her till she flushed all over. His eyes widened beneath thick dark lashes and she saw they were green. The deep, hard green of emeralds. Luisa read shock in his expression. And, she could have sworn, dismay.

Seconds later he'd masked his emotions and his expression was unreadable. Only a slight bunching of sleek black eyebrows hinted he wasn't happy.

'Ms *Luisa* Hardwicke?'

He pronounced her name the way her mother

had, with a soft s and a lilt that turned the mundane into something pretty.

Premonition clamped a chill hand at the back of her neck. The accent *had* to be a coincidence. That other world was beyond her reach now.

Luisa wiped the worst of the dirt off her hand and stepped forward, arm outstretched. It was time to take charge of this situation. 'And you are?'

He hesitated for a moment, then her fingers were engulfed in his. He bowed, almost as if to kiss her hand. The gesture was charming and outlandish. It sent a squiggle of reaction through her, making her breath falter. Especially as his warm, powerful hand still held hers.

Heat scalded her face and she was actually grateful for the smearing of dirt that concealed it.

He straightened and she had to arch her neck to meet his glittering scrutiny. From this angle he seemed all imposing, austere lines that spoke of unyielding strength.

Luisa blinked and drew a shaky breath, trying to ignore the butterflies swirling in her stomach and think sensibly.

'I am Raul of Maritz.' He said it simply but with such assurance she could almost imagine a blare of trumpet fanfare in the background. 'Prince Raul.'

* * *

Raul watched her stiffen and felt the ripple of shock jolt through her. She yanked her hand free and took a step back, arms crossing protectively over her chest.

His mind clicked up a gear as interest sparked. *Not* the welcome he usually received. Fawning excitement was more common.

'Why are you here?' This time the throaty edge to her words wasn't gruff. It made her sound vulnerable and feminine.

Feminine! He hadn't realised she was a woman!

From her husky voice to her muddy boots, square overalls and battered hat that shadowed her grimy face, she had as much feminine appeal as a cabbage. She still hadn't removed the hat. And that walk! Stiff as an automaton.

He froze, imagining her in Maritzian society where protocol and exquisite manners were prized. This was worse than he'd feared. And there was no way out.

Not if he was to claim his throne and safeguard his country.

He clenched his teeth, silently berating the archaic legalities that bound him in this catch-22.

When he was king there'd be some changes.

'I asked what you're doing on my land.' No mistaking the animosity in her tone. More and more intriguing.

'My apologies.' Automatically he smiled, smoothing over his lapse. It was no excuse that the shock of seeing her distracted him. 'We have important matters to discuss.'

He waited for her answering smile. For a relaxation of her rigid stance. There was none.

'We have nothing to discuss.' Beneath the mud her neat chin angled up.

She was giving *him* the brush-off? It was absurd!

'Nevertheless, it's true.'

He waited for her to invite him in. She stood unmoving, staring up balefully. Impatience stirred.

And more, a wave of distaste at the fate that decreed he had to take this woman under his wing. Turn this unpromising material into—

'I'd like you to leave.'

Raul stiffened in indignation. At the same time curiosity intensified. He wished he could see her without that mask of mud.

'I've travelled from my homeland in Europe to speak with you.'

'That's impossible, I tell you. I have no—'

'Far from being impossible, I made the trip for that sole purpose.' Raul drew himself up and took a pace closer, letting his superior height send a silent message. When he spoke again it was in a tone that brooked no opposition. 'I'm not leaving until we've concluded our business.'

Luisa's stomach twisted in knots and her nerves stretched to breaking point as she hurried through the house back to the veranda where she'd left her visitor.

The crown prince of Maritz, her mother's homeland, here at her house! *This couldn't be good.*

She'd tried to send him away, turn her back rather than face anyone from that place. The memories were too poisonous. But he'd been frighteningly immovable. A single look at that steely jaw told her she wouldn't succeed.

Besides, she needed to know why he was here.

Now, armoured as best she could manage by scouring hot water and clean clothes, she tried to stifle rising panic.

What did he want?

He filled up her veranda with his larger than life presence, making her feel small and insignificant. His spare features reminded her of pictures of the old king in his youth—impossibly handsome with his high cut cheekbones and proud bearing. From his top notch tailoring to his air of command, this man was *someone*.

Yet royalty didn't just pop in to visit.

Disquiet shivered through her. A shadow of the stormy past.

He turned to her. Instantly she felt at a disadvantage. With those chiselled aristocratic features and that uncompromising air of maleness he was… stunning. Despite her wariness, heat ricocheted through her abdomen.

His eyes narrowed. Luisa's heartbeat pattered out of kilter and her mouth dried. With a jolt of shock she realised it was the man himself, as much as his identity that disturbed her.

Luisa laced her fingers rather than straighten her loose shirt, her only clean one after weeks of rain. She wished she could meet him on equal terms, dressed to the nines. But her budget didn't run to new clothes. Or a new hairdryer.

She smoothed damp locks from her face and pushed back her shoulders, ignoring the way her stomach somersaulted. She refused to be intimidated in her own home.

'I was admiring your view,' he said. 'It's lovely countryside.'

Luisa cast her eyes over the familiar rolling hills. She appreciated the natural beauty, but it had been a long time since she'd found time to enjoy it.

'If you'd seen it two months ago after years of

drought you wouldn't have been so impressed.' She drew a deep breath, fighting down the sick certainty that this man was trouble. Her skin crawled with nervous tension but she refused to let him see. 'Won't you come in?'

She moved to open the door but with a long stride he beat her to it, gesturing for her to precede him.

Luisa wasn't used to having doors opened for her. That was why she flushed.

She inhaled a subtle, exotic scent that went straight to her head. Luisa bit her lip as tingles shot to her toes. None of the men she knew looked, sounded or smelled as good as Raul of Maritz.

'Please, take a seat.' She gestured jerkily to the scrubbed kitchen table. Luisa hadn't had a chance to move the buckets and tarpaulins from the lounge room, where they'd staved off the leaks from the last downpour.

Besides, she'd long ago learnt that aristocratic birth was no measure of worth. He could sit where her friends and business partners met.

'Of course.' He pulled out a chair and sank into it with as much aplomb as if it were a plushly padded throne. His presence filled the room.

She lifted the kettle, her movements jerky as she stifled hostility. She needed to hear him out. 'Would you like coffee or tea?'

'No, thank you.' His face was unreadable.

Luisa's pulse sped as she met his unblinking regard. Reluctantly she slid into a chair opposite him, forcing herself into stillness.

'So, Your Highness. What can I do for you?'

For a moment longer he regarded her, then he leaned forward a fraction. 'It's not what you can do for me.' His voice was deep, mellow and hypnotic, holding a promise to which she instinctively responded despite her wariness. 'This is about what I can do for you.'

Beware of strangers promising gifts. The little voice inside sent a tremor of disquiet skidding through her.

Years before she'd received promises of wonderful gifts. The future had seemed a magical, glittering land. Yet it had all been a hollow sham. She'd learned distrust the hard way—not once but twice.

'Really?' Her face felt stiff and she found it hard to swallow.

He nodded. 'First I need to confirm you're the only child of Thomas Bevan Hardwicke and Margarite Luisa Carlotta Hardwicke.'

Luisa froze, alarm stirring. He sounded like a lawyer about to break bad news. The voice of warning in her head grew more strident. Surely her ties with Maritz had been completely severed years ago.

'That's right, though I can't see—'

'It pays to be sure. Tell me—' he leaned back in his seat but his eyes never wavered from hers '—how much do you know about my country? About its government and states?'

Luisa fought to remain calm as painful memories surged. This meeting had a nightmare quality. She wanted to scream at him to get to the point before her stretched nerves gave way. But that glittering gaze was implacable. He'd do this his way. She'd known men like him before. She gritted her teeth.

'Enough.' *More than she wanted.* 'It's an alpine kingdom. A democracy with a parliament and a king.'

He nodded. 'My father the king died recently. I will be crowned in a few months.'

'I'm sorry for your loss,' Luisa murmured, struggling to make sense of this. *Why was he here, interrogating her?* The question beat at her brain.

'Thank you.' He paused. 'And Ardissia?'

Luisa's fingers clenched as she fought impatience. She shot him a challenging look. He was like a charming bulldozer, with that polite smile barely cloaking his determination to get his own way.

'It's a province of Maritz, with its own hereditary prince who owes loyalty to the King of Maritz.' Her mouth twisted. 'My mother came from there, *as I'm sure you know.*'

She shivered, cold sweeping up from her toes and wrapping around her heart as bitter memories claimed her.

'Now, my turn for a question.' She planted her palms on the table and leaned forward, fixing him with a stare. 'Why are you here?'

Luisa waited, her heart thudding hectically, watching him survey her beneath lowered brows. He shifted in his seat. Suddenly she wondered if he were uncomfortable too.

'I came to find you.' His expression made her heartbeat speed to a pounding gallop.

'Why?'

'The Prince of Ardissia is dead. I'm here to tell you you're his heiress, Princess Luisa of Ardissia.'

CHAPTER TWO

RAUL watched her pale beneath her tan. Her eyes rounded and she swayed in her seat. Was she going to faint?

Great. A highly strung female!

He thrust aside the fact that anyone would be overcome. That his anger at this diabolical situation made him unreasonable.

She wasn't the only one whose life had been turned on its head! For years Raul had steered his own course, making every decision. Being fettered like this was outrageous.

But the alternative—to turn his back on his people and the life to which he'd devoted himself—was unthinkable.

'Are you all right?'

'Of course.' Her tone was sharp but her eyes were dazed.

They were surprisingly fine eyes, seen without that shadowing hat. Blue-grey a moment ago, now they sparkled brilliant azure. Like a clear summer sky in the Maritzian Alps. The sort of eyes a man could lose himself in.

She blinked and shifted her gaze and Raul was astonished to feel a pang of disappointment.

He watched her gnaw her lip. When she looked up and flushed to find him watching, he noticed the ripe contours of her mouth. With the grime washed away, her features were pleasant, regular and fairly attractive.

If you liked the artless, scrubbed bare style.

Raul preferred his women sophisticated and well groomed.

What sort of woman didn't take the time to style her hair? Pale and damply combed off her face, it even looked lopsided. Anyone less fitted for this—

'I can't be his heir!' She sounded almost accusing.

His brows rose. As if he'd waste precious time here on a whim!

'Believe me, it's true.'

She blinked and he had the sense there was more going on behind her azure eyes than simple surprise.

'How is it possible?' She sounded as if she spoke to herself.

'Here.' Raul opened the briefcase Lukas had

brought. 'Here's your grandfather's will and your family tree.'

He'd planned for his secretary, Lukas, to take her through this. But he'd changed his mind the moment he saw Luisa Hardwicke and how unprepared she was for this role. Better do this himself. The fewer who dealt with her at this early stage the better.

Raul suppressed a grimace. What had begun as a delicate mission now had unlimited potential for disaster. Imagine the headlines if the press saw her as she was! He wouldn't allow the Maritzian crown to be the focus of rabid media gossip again. Especially at this difficult time.

He strode round the table and spread the papers before her.

She shifted in her seat as if his presence contaminated her. Raul stiffened. Women were usually eager to get close.

'Here's your mother.' He modulated his tone reassuringly. 'Above her, your grandfather, the last prince.'

She lifted her head from examining the family tree. Again the impact of that bright gaze hit him. He'd swear he felt it like a rumbling echo inside his chest.

'Why isn't my uncle inheriting? Or my cousin, Marissa?'

'You're the last of your family.'

Her brow puckered. 'She must have been so young. That's awful.'

'Yes.' The accident was a tragic waste of life. And it altered the succession.

She shook her head. 'But I'm not part of the family! My mother was disinherited when she fell in love with an Australian and refused to marry the man her father chose.'

She knew about that? Did that explain her animosity?

'Your grandfather blustered but he never disinherited her. We only discovered that recently when his will was read.' The Prince of Ardissia had been an irascible tartar but he had too much pride in his bloodline to cut off a direct descendant. 'You're definitely eligible to inherit.'

How much easier life would be if she weren't!

If there were no Ardissian princess he wouldn't be in this appalling situation.

'I tell you it's impossible!' She leaned forward, her brow pleating as she scanned the papers.

The scent of lavender wafted to him. Raul inhaled, intrigued. He was used to the perfectly balanced notes of the most expensive perfumes. Yet this simple fragrance was strangely appealing.

'It *can't* be right.' She spoke again. 'He disinherited me too. We were told so!'

Startled, he looked down to find her eyes blazing up at him. Her chin was angled in the air and for the first time there was colour in her cheeks.

She looked…pretty. In an unsophisticated way.

And she knew more than he'd expected. Fascinating.

'Despite what you were told, you're his heiress. You inherit his fortune and responsibilities.' He summoned an encouraging smile. 'I've come to take you home.'

'Home?' Luisa shot to her feet, the chair screeching across the floor. 'This is my home! I belong here.' She gestured to the cosy kitchen she'd known all her life.

She fought a sense of unreality. This had to be an appalling mistake.

From the moment he'd mentioned Ardissia and Maritz bitter recollection had cramped her belly and clouded her brain. It had taken a superhuman effort to hear him out.

'Not any more.' Across the scrubbed table he smiled.

He really was unbelievably good-looking.

Until you looked into those cool eyes. Had he thought her too unaware to notice his smile didn't reach his eyes?

'You've got a new life ahead of you. Your world will change for ever.' His smile altered, became somehow more intimate, and to her surprise Luisa felt a trickle of unfamiliar warmth spread through her body.

How had that happened?

'You'll have wealth, position, prestige—the best of everything. You'll live a life of luxury, as a princess.'

A princess.

The words reverberated in Luisa's skull. Nausea rose.

At sixteen she'd heard those same words. It had been like a dream come true. What girl wouldn't be excited to discover a royal bloodline and a doting grandfather promising a life of excitement and privilege?

Luisa's heart clutched as she remembered her mother, pale but bravely smiling, seated at this table, telling her she had to make up her own mind about her future. Saying that, though she'd turned her back on that life, it was Luisa's choice if she wanted to discover her birthright.

And, like the innocent she was, Luisa had gone. Lured by the fairy tale fantasy of a picture book kingdom.

Reality had been brutally different. By the time she'd rejected what her grandfather offered and made her own way home, she'd been only too grateful he hadn't publicly presented her as his kin. That he'd kept her a cloistered guest during her 'probation' period. Only her closest family knew she'd ever been tempted by the old man's false promises of a joyful family reunion.

She'd been naïve but no more.

Now she knew too much about the ugly reality of that aristocratic society, where birth and connections mattered more than love and common decency. If her grandfather's actions hadn't been enough, she only had to recall the man she'd thought she'd loved. How he'd schemed to seduce her when he realised her secret identity. All because of his ambition.

Luisa's stomach heaved and she reached out blindly for the table, shaking her head to clear the nightmarish recollections.

'I don't want to be a princess.'

Silence. Slowly she turned. Prince Raul's hooded eyes were wide, impatience obliterated by shock.

'You can't be serious,' he said finally, his voice thickening with that appealing accent.

'Believe me, I was never more so.'

Revulsion filled Luisa as she remembered her grandfather. He'd invited her to join him so he could groom her into the sort of princess he wanted. To do his bidding without question. To be the sort his daughter had failed to be.

At first Luisa had been blind to the fact he merely wanted a pawn to manipulate, not a granddaughter to love.

He'd shown his true colours when news arrived of her mother's terminal illness. He'd refused Luisa's tearful, desperate pleas to return. Instead he'd issued an ultimatum—that she break off all contact with her parents or give up her new life. As for Luisa's begging that he fund further medical treatment, he'd snarled at her for wasting time on the woman who'd turned her back on his world.

That heartless betrayal, so blatant, so overwhelming, still sickened Luisa to the core.

That was who she was heir to! A cruel, ruthless tyrant. No wonder she'd vowed not to have anything to do with her bigoted, blue-blooded family.

She recalled her grandfather bellowing his displeasure at her ingratitude. At her inability to be what he wanted, play the part.

A hand on her arm tugged her from her thoughts. She looked up into a searing gaze. Black eyebrows tilted in a V and Raul's nostrils flared as if scenting fear.

This close he was arresting. Her stomach plunged in freefall as she stared back. Tingling sensation spread from his touch.

Luisa swallowed and his eyes followed the movement.

The intensity of his regard scared her. The beat of her blood was like thunder in her ears. She felt unprotected beneath a gaze that had lost its distance and now seemed to flare with unexpected heat.

'What is it? What are you thinking?' Gone was the smooth tone. His words were staccato sharp.

Luisa drew a shaky breath, disoriented by the arcing heat that snapped and shimmered in the air between them. By the hazy sense of familiarity she felt with this handsome stranger.

'I'm thinking you should let me go.'

Immediately he stepped back, his hand dropping. 'Forgive me. For a moment you looked faint.'

She nodded. She'd felt queasy. That explained her unsteadiness. It had nothing to do with his touch.

The electricity sparking between them was imaginary.

He thrust a hand through his immaculately combed hair as if, for an instant, he too felt that disturbing sensation. But then his dark locks fell back into perfect position and he was again cool, clear-eyed and commanding.

Swiftly Luisa turned to grab a glass. She gulped down cold water, hoping to restore a semblance of normality. She felt as if she'd been wrung inside out.

Finally she willed her scrambled thoughts into order. It didn't help that she sensed Prince Raul's gaze skewer her like an insect on a pin.

Setting her jaw, she turned.

He leaned against the dresser, arms folded and one ankle casually resting on the other. He looked unattainably sexy and a little scary. His brow was furrowed as if something perplexed him, but that only emphasised the strength of his features.

'When you've had time to absorb the news, you'll see going to Maritz is the sensible thing.'

'Thank you, but I've already absorbed the news.' Did he have any idea how patronising he sounded? Annoyance sizzled in her blood.

He didn't move but his big body was no longer relaxed. His folded arms with their bunched muscles drew her eyes. Suddenly he looked predatory rather than suavely elegant.

Her skin prickled.

'The money doesn't tempt you?' His mouth compressed. Obviously he thought money outweighed everything else.

Just like her grandfather and his cronies.

Luisa opened her mouth, then snapped it shut as her dazed brain cells finally revved into action.

Money!

In her shock that hadn't even registered. She thought of the looming debts, repairs they'd postponed, Sam's outdated milking machine and her own rattletrap car. The list was endless.

'How much money?' She wanted nothing of the high society position. But the cash…

The prince unfolded his arms and named a sum that made her head spin. She braced herself against the table.

'When do I get it?' Her voice was scratchy with shock.

Did she imagine a flash of satisfaction in those dark green eyes?

'You're princess whether you use the title or not. Nothing can alter that.' He paused. 'But there are conditions on inheriting your wealth. You must settle in Maritz and take up your royal obligations.'

Luisa's shoulders slumped. What he suggested was impossible. She'd rejected that world for her own sanity. Accepting would be a betrayal of herself and all she held dear.

'I can't.'

'Of course you can. I'll make the arrangements.'

'Don't you listen?' Luisa gripped the table so hard her bones ached. 'I'm not going!' Life in that cold, cruel society would kill her. 'This is my home. My roots are here.'

He shook his head, straightening to stand tall and imposing. The room shrank and despite her anger she felt his formidable magnetism tug at her.

'You have roots in Maritz too. What have you got here but hard work and poverty? In my country you'll have a privileged life, mixing in the most elite circles.'

How he sounded like her snobbish grandfather.

'I prefer the circles I mix in.' Fire skirled in her belly at his condescension. 'The people I love are here.'

He scowled. 'A man?' He took a step closer and, involuntarily, Luisa retreated a pace before the fierce light in his eyes.

'No, my friends. And my father's brother and his wife.' Sam and Mary, almost a generation older than Luisa's parents, had been like doting grandparents through her sunny childhood and the darkest days. She wouldn't leave them, ageing and in debt, for a glamorous, empty life far away.

The sharp-eyed man before her didn't look impressed.

Had her grandfather once looked like Prince Raul? Proud, determined, good-looking and boy, didn't he know it!

Standing there, radiating impatience, Raul embodied everything she'd learned to despise.

Determination surged anew.

'Thank you for coming to tell me in person.' She drew herself up, level with his proud chin, and folded his papers with quick, precise movements. 'But you'll have to find someone else to inherit.' She breathed deep. 'I'll see you out.'

Raul's mouth tightened as the chopper lifted.

Thrilled! Luisa Hardwicke had been anything but. Just as well he'd told her only about her inheritance, not the more challenging aspects of her new role. She'd been so skittish it was wiser to break that news later.

He'd never met a more stubborn woman. She'd all but thrown him out!

Indignation danced in his veins and tightened his fists.

Something motivated her that he didn't know

about. He needed to discover what it was. More, he had to discover the trigger that would make her change her mind.

For an instant back there he'd been tempted simply to kidnap her. The blood of generations of warriors and robber barons as well as monarchs flowed in his veins. It would have been easy to scoop her up in his arms and sequester her till she saw reason. *So satisfying.*

An image of Luisa Hardwicke filled his mind. She stared defiantly up with flashing cerulean eyes.

Raul recalled her shirt lifting when she reached for a glass, revealing her lusciously curved bottom in snug jeans. The feminine shape outlined by her shirt when she moved. A shape at odds with his original impression.

Fire streaked through Raul's belly.

Perhaps there would be compensations after all.

Luisa Hardwicke had a wholesome prettiness that appealed far more than it ought. He'd made it his business these last eight years to surround himself only with glamorous, sophisticated women who understood his needs.

He grimaced, facing a truth he rarely acknowledged. That if he'd once had a weakness it had been for the sort of forthright honesty and fresh openness she projected.

The sort he'd once believed in.

Sordid reality had cured him of any such frailty. Yet being with her was like hearing an echo of his past, remembering fragments of dreams he'd once held. Dreams now shattered beyond repair by deceit and betrayal.

And, despite his indignation, he responded to her pride, her pluck.

It was an inconvenience that complicated his plans. Yet perversely he admired the challenge she represented. What a change from the compliant, eager women he knew! In other circumstances he'd applaud her stance.

Besides, he saw now, a spineless nonentity would never have been suitable for what was to come. Or so surprisingly appealing.

Raul tugged his mind back to business. He needed a lever to ensure she saw sense. Failure wasn't an option when his nation depended on him.

'Lukas, you said the farming co-op is in debt?'

'Yes sir, heavily so. I'm amazed it's still running.'

Raul looked back at the tiny speck that was her home. A sliver of regret pierced him. He'd wanted to avoid coercion but she left him no choice.

'Buy the debts. Immediately. I want it settled today.'

* * *

The roar of a helicopter brought Luisa's head up.

It couldn't be. After rejecting her inheritance yesterday there was no reason for her path and Prince Raul's to cross again. Yet she was drawn inexorably to the window. It couldn't be but it was. Prince Raul—here!

To Luisa's annoyance, her heart pattered faster as she watched his long, powerful frame vault from the chopper.

Twenty-four hours had given her time to assure herself he wasn't nearly as imposing as she remembered.

She'd been wrong.

Luisa had searched him on the web yesterday, learning his reputation for hard work and wealth. The reports also referred to discreet liaisons with gorgeous women.

Yet no photos did justice to his impact in the flesh. Her breath caught as he loped up the steps. Good thing she was immune.

'Luisa.' He stood before her, wide shoulders filling the open doorway, his voice smooth like dark chocolate with a hint of spice as he lingered on her name.

A tremor rippled through her as she responded to the exotic sound of her name on his tongue. It maddened her that she should react so. She pulled herself together, fiercely quelling a riot of unfamiliar emotions.

'Your Highness.' She gripped the door hard. 'Why are you here? We finished our business yesterday.' Surely he had VIPs to see, deals to forge, women to seduce.

He bent over her hand in another courtly almost-kiss that knotted her stomach. She had to remind herself not to be impressed by surface charm. *Been there, done that.*

Yet her gaze riveted on his austerely handsome face as he straightened. The flash of green fire in his eyes sent tendrils of heat curling through her. His fingers squeezed and her pulse accelerated.

'Call me Raul.'

It went against the grain but to refuse would be churlish.

'Raul.' It was crazy but she could almost taste his name in her mouth, like a rich, full-bodied wine.

'Aren't you going to invite me in?' One dark eyebrow rose lazily as if her obstinacy amused him. She bit down on a rude response. He must have good reason to return. The sooner she heard it the sooner he'd go.

'Please, come in.' She led the way to the lounge room, ignoring the jitter of nerves in her stomach.

Instead of making himself comfortable, he took

up a position in front of the window. A command-ing position, she noticed uneasily as premonition skittered across her nape.

She didn't like the glint in his eye or his wide-legged stance, as if claiming her territory for his own. She stood facing him, refusing to be domi-nated.

'You haven't changed your mind?'

She lifted her chin a fraction. 'Not if the cash comes with strings attached.'

Desperate as she was for money, she couldn't agree.

She'd spent yesterday afternoon consulting her solicitor. There *must* be a way to access some of the money she was in line to inherit without giving up her life here. She didn't trust Raul, a man with his own agenda, to be straight with her on that.

It was too soon to know, but the possibility she could negotiate enough funds to give the co-op the boost it needed had given her a better night's sleep than she'd had in ages. It buoyed her now, strengthening her confidence.

'Can I persuade you to reconsider?' His mouth turned up in the barest hint of a smile, yet even that should have come with a health warning.

Her breath sawed in her throat and her pulse quickened.

Luisa thought of the enquiries being made on her behalf. She'd be a fool to give in to his preposterous suggestion. 'Absolutely not.' The very thought of accepting made her ill.

'That's unfortunate.' He paused so long her nerves stretched taut. 'Very unfortunate.' He looked grim.

Finally he reached into his jacket pocket. 'In that case, these are for you.'

Bewildered, Luisa accepted the papers. 'You want me to sign away my inheritance?' She'd sign nothing without legal advice.

He shook his head. 'Take your time. They're self-explanatory.'

Confused, she skimmed the papers. Unlike yesterday's, these weren't rich parchment. They looked more like the loan documents that were the bane of her life.

Luisa forced herself to concentrate. Hard to do with his stare on her. When finally she began to understand, the world spun around her.

'You've bought the co-op's debts.' Disbelieving, she shuffled the papers, eyes goggling. 'All of them!'

And in one day. Each paper had yesterday's date. Was it even possible?

Bewildered, she looked up. The gravity of his expression convinced her more than the typed words.

Luisa sank abruptly onto the arm of a chair, her knees too wobbly to take her weight, her breath choppy.

What strings had he pulled to manage that in a single day? Luisa couldn't conceive of such power. Yet, staring up at the man before her, she realised he wielded authority as easily as she managed a milking machine.

The realisation dried her mouth.

'Why?' Her voice was a hoarse rasp.

He paced closer, looming between her and the light from the window. 'On the day you sign the documents accepting your inheritance, I'll make a gift of them. You can rip them into confetti.'

Relief poured through her veins so suddenly she shook.

He was so obstinate! He still didn't accept her rejection. No doubt he thought it embarrassing that the heir to a royal title was neck-deep in debt.

It was a generous gesture. One she'd compensate him for if she found a way to access the funds.

'But I'm not going. I'm staying here.'

'You won't.'

Had anyone ever denied him what he wanted?

Impatient energy radiated off him. And that chin—she'd never seen a more determined face.

Luisa stood. She needed to assert herself and end

this nonsense. It was time he accepted she knew her mind. 'I've got no plans to leave.'

He held her gaze as the seconds stretched out. His expression didn't change but a frisson of anxiety skipped up her back, like a spider dancing on her vertebrae.

'Knowing how committed you are to the well-being of your family and friends, I'm sure you'll change your mind.' His voice held steel beneath the deep velvet inflection. 'Unless you want them to lose everything.'

He spoke so matter-of-factly it took a moment to register the threat.

Luisa's face froze and a gasp caught inside as her throat closed convulsively.

Blackmail?

She opened her mouth but no sound emerged. Paper cascaded to the floor from her trembling hands.

'You...can't be serious!'

Slowly he shook his head. 'Never more so, Luisa.'

'Don't call me that!' The way he said her name, with the same lilting accent her mother had used, was like a travesty of a familiar endearment.

'Princess Luisa, then.'

She took a furious step forward, her hands clenching in frustration. 'This has to be a joke.'

But no humour showed on his stern features. 'You can't foreclose! You'd destroy the livelihood of a dozen families.' And her father's dream. What she had worked for most of her life.

After she'd returned home to nurse her mother, Luisa had never found time to go back and finish school. Instead she'd stayed on to help her father, who'd never fully recovered from the loss of his wife.

'The decision is yours. You can save them, if they mean as much as you claim.'

He meant it! The grim determination in his granite-set jaw was nothing to the resolution in his glittering eyes.

'But...*why?*' Luisa shook her head, trying to find sense in a world turned topsy-turvy. 'You can find another heir, someone who'd be thrilled to live the life you're offering.' Someone happy to give up her soul for the riches he promised. 'I'm not princess material!'

The gleam in his eyes suggested he agreed.

'There *is* no one else, Luisa. You are the princess.'

'You can't dictate my future!' Luisa planted her hands on her hips, letting defiance mask her sudden fear. 'Why are you getting so personally involved?'

When her grandfather had made contact it had been through emissaries. He hadn't come to her. Yet Raul as crown prince was far more important than her grandfather.

He took her hand before she could snatch it away. Heat engulfed her, radiating from his touch and searing her skin even as his intentions chilled her marrow.

'I have a stake in your future,' he murmured.

Automatically she jerked up her chin. 'Really?' The word emerged defiantly.

'A very personal stake.' His grip firmed, all except for his thumb, which stroked gently across her palm, sending little judders of awareness through her. 'Not only are you the Ardissian heiress, you're destined to be Queen of Maritz.' He paused, eyes locking with hers.

'That's why I'm here. To take you back as my bride.'

CHAPTER THREE

LUISA watched his firm lips shape the word 'bride'. Her head reeled.

There was no laughter in his eyes. No wildness hinting at insanity. Just a steady certainty that locked the protest in her mouth.

Her lungs cramped from lack of oxygen as her breath escaped in a whoosh. She lurched forward, dragging in air. He grasped her hand tight and reached for her shoulder as if to support her.

Violently she wrenched away, breaking his grip and retreating to stand, panting, beside the window.

'Don't touch me!'

His eyes narrowed to slits of green fire and she sensed that behind his calm exterior lurked a man of volatile passions.

'Explain. Now!' she said when she'd caught her breath.

'Perhaps you'd better sit.'

So he could tower over her? No, thank you! 'I prefer to stand.' Even if her legs felt like unset jelly.

'As you wish.' Why did it sound like he granted her a special favour in her own house?

He had royal condescension down to an art form.

'You were going to explain why you need to marry.' For the life of her, Luisa couldn't say 'marry me'.

His look told her he didn't miss the omission.

'To ascend the throne I must be married.' At her stare he continued. 'It's an old law, aimed to ensure an unbroken royal lineage.'

A tremor scudded through her at the idea of 'ensuring the royal lineage'. *With him.*

It didn't matter how handsome he was. She'd learnt looks could hide a black heart. It was the inner man that counted. From what she'd seen, Raul was as proud, opinionated and selfish as her detested grandfather.

The way he looked when she challenged him— jaw tight and eyes flashing malachite sparks, was warning enough.

Luisa's heartbeat pounded so hard she had trouble hearing his next words.

'It's tradition that the crown prince take a bride from one of Maritz's principalities. When we were in our teens a contract was drawn up for my marriage to your cousin, Marissa, Princess of Ardissia. But Marissa died soon after.'

'I'm sorry,' Luisa said gruffly. She searched his features for regret but couldn't read anything. Didn't he feel *something* for his fiancée who'd died?

She pursed her lips. Obviously the heartless arranged marriage was still alive and thriving in Maritz!

'After that I was in no hurry to tie myself in marriage. But when my father died recently it was time to find another bride.'

'So you could inherit.' Luisa shivered, remembering that world where marriages were dynastic contracts, devoid of love. She crossed her arms protectively. How could he be so sanguine about it?

'My plans were curtailed when your grandfather's will was read and we discovered you would inherit. Before then, given what he'd said about disowning your mother, your branch of the family didn't feature in our considerations.'

He made them sound like tiresome complications in his grand design! Indignation rose anew.

'What has the will got to do with your marriage?'

'The contract is binding, Luisa.' He loomed far too close. Her lungs constricted, making her breathing choppy.

'But how?' Luisa paced away, urgently needing space. 'If Marissa is—'

'Everyone, including the genealogists and lawyers, believed your grandfather's line would die with him. The news he had a granddaughter who hadn't been disinherited was a bombshell.' He didn't look as if the news had pleased him. 'You should be thankful we were able to find you before the media got the story. You'd have had press camped here around the clock.'

'You're overdramatising.' Luisa's hands curled tight as she forced down growing panic. 'I've got nothing to do with your wedding.'

One dark eyebrow winged upwards. 'The antiquated style of the contract means I'm bound to marry the Princess of Ardissia.' He paused, his mouth a slash of pure displeasure. *Whoever she is.'*

'You're out of your mind!' Luisa retreated a frantic step, her stomach a churning mess. This truly *was* a nightmare. 'I never signed any contract!'

'It doesn't matter. The document is legal.' His lips twisted. 'The best minds in the country can't find a way out of it.'

She shook her head, her hair falling across her face as she backed up against the window. 'No way! No matter what your contract says, you can't take me back there as—'

'My bride?' The words dropped into echoing silence. Luisa heard them repeat over and over in her numbed brain, like a never-ending ripple spreading in a still, icy pool.

'Believe me; I'll do what's necessary to claim my throne.' His chin lifted regally, making clear what he hadn't put in words: that he didn't wish to marry someone so far beneath him. Someone so unappealing.

Why was he so desperate? Did power mean so much?

Luisa choked on rising anger. Twenty-four years old and she'd received two marriage offers—both from ambitious men who saw her as nothing but a means to acquire power! Why couldn't she meet a caring, honest man who'd love her for herself? She felt soiled and cheap.

'You expect me to give up my life and marry you, a total stranger, so you can become king?' What century had he dropped out of? 'You're talking antiquated nonsense.'

His look grazed like shards of ice on bare skin. 'It may be antiquated but I must marry.'

She jutted her chin. 'Marry someone else!'

Something dangerous and dark flashed in his

eyes. But when he spoke his words were measured. She sensed he hung onto his control by a thread.

'If I could I would. If you hadn't existed or if you'd already married, the contract would be void and I could choose another bride.'

As if choosing a wife took a minimum of time and effort!

Though in his case it might. With his looks, sexual magnetism and wealth there'd be lots of women eager to overlook the fact they tied themselves to a power hungry egotist!

His deep voice sent a tremor rippling through her overwrought body. 'There's no more time to find a way out. I need to be married within the constitutional time limit or I can't inherit.'

'Why should I care?' Luisa rubbed her hands up chilled arms, trying to restore warmth. 'I don't even know you.'

And what she did know she didn't like.

He shrugged and unwillingly Luisa saw how the fluid movement drew attention to those powerful shoulders. The sort of shoulders that belonged on a surf lifesaver or an outback farmer, not a privileged aristocrat.

'I'm the best person for the kingship. Some would say the only suitable one. I've trained a lifetime for it.'

'Others could learn.'

He shook his head. 'Not now. Not in time. There was unrest in the last years of my father's reign. That's growing. A strong king is what the country needs.'

The sizzle in his eyes stopped her breath.

'That leaves only one option.'

She was his only option!

'I don't care!' Cool glass pressed against her back as he took a pace towards her and she stepped back. 'Let them crown someone else. I'm not a sacrificial lamb for the slaughter.'

His lips curled in a knowing smile that should have repelled her. Yet her heart hammered as she watched his eyes light with a gleam that warmed her from tip to toe.

'You think marriage to me would be a hardship?' His voice dropped to a low pitch that feathered like a sultry breeze across her suddenly flushed skin. 'That I don't know how to please a woman?'

Luisa swallowed hard, using her hands to anchor herself to the windowsill behind her rather than be drawn towards the glittering green gaze that seemed now to promise unspoken delights.

He was far more dangerous than she'd realised.

'Be assured, Luisa, that you will find pleasure in our union. You have my word on it.'

A beat of power, of heat, pulsed between them and she knew how an animal felt, mesmerised by a predator.

'The answer is still no,' she whispered hoarsely, shocked at the need to force down a betraying weakness that made her respond to his sensual promise. Why did her dormant hormones suddenly jangle into life around *him*?

For a long moment they stood, adversaries in a silent battle of wills.

'Then, sadly, you leave me no choice.' The fire in his eyes was doused as if it had never been. A flicker of what might have been regret shadowed his gaze then disappeared. 'Just remember that decision, and the outcome, are entirely yours.'

Already he turned away. Only her hand on his elbow stopped him.

'What do you mean?' Fear was a sour tang in her mouth.

He didn't turn. 'I have business to finalise before I leave. Some farms to dispose of.'

Panic surged. Luisa's fingers tightened like a claw on the fine wool of his suit. She stepped round to look up into his stern face.

'You can't foreclose! They haven't done anything to you.'

His stare pinioned her. He shook off her hand.

'In a choice between your relatives and my country there is no contest.' He inclined his head. 'Goodbye, Luisa.'

'I'm sure Mademoiselle will be happy with this new style. A little shorter, a little more chic. Yes?'

Luisa dragged herself from her troubled reverie and met the eyes of the young Frenchwoman in the mirror. Clearly the stylist was excited at being summoned to the Prince's exclusive Parisian residence. Unlike the nail technician who'd barely resisted snorting her displeasure when Luisa had refused false nails, knowing she'd never manage them. Or the haughty couturier who'd taken her measurements with barely concealed contempt for Luisa's clothes.

The hair stylist hadn't been daunted at the prospect of working on someone as ordinary as Luisa.

Perhaps she liked a challenge.

'I'm sure it will be lovely.' Another time Luisa would have been thrilled, having her hair done by someone with such flair and enthusiasm. But not today, just hours after Raul's private jet had touched down in Paris.

It had all happened too fast. Even her goodbyes to Sam and a tearful Mary, crying over the happy news that Luisa was taking up her long lost inheritance.

How she wished she were with them now. Back in the world she knew, where she belonged.

Luisa gritted her teeth, remembering how Raul had taken the initiative from her even in her farewells.

When she'd gone to break the news it was to find he'd been there first. Her family and friends were already agog with the story of Luisa finally taking her 'rightful place' as a princess. And with news their debts were to be cancelled.

Yet Luisa had at least asserted herself in demanding Raul install a capable farm manager in her place to get the co-op on its feet. She refused to leave her friends short-handed.

In the face of their pleasure, Luisa had felt almost selfish, longing to stay, when so much good came out of her departure. Yet she'd left part of herself behind.

Her family and friends would have been distraught, knowing why she left. They wouldn't have touched the Prince's money if they knew the truth. But she couldn't do that to them. She couldn't ruin them for her pride.

Or her deep-seated fear of what awaited her in Maritz.

She shivered when she thought of entering Raul's world. Being with a man who should repel her, yet who—

'These layers will complement the jaw line, see? And make this lovely hair easier to manage.'

Luisa nodded vaguely.

'And, you will forgive me saying, cut even on both sides suits you better, yes?'

Luisa looked up, catching a sparkle in the other woman's eye. Heat seeped under her skin as she remembered her previous lopsided cut. She tilted her chin.

'My friend wants to become a hairdresser. She practised on me.'

'Her instincts were good, but the execution...' The other woman made one last judicious snip, then stepped away. 'Voila! What do you think?'

For the first time Luisa really focused. She kept staring as the stylist used a mirror to reveal her new look from all sides.

It wasn't a new look. It was a new woman!

Her overgrown hair was now a gleaming silky fall that danced and slid around her neck as she turned, yet always fell sleekly back into place. It was shorter, barely reaching her shoulders, but shaped now to the contours of her face. Dull dark blonde had been transformed into a burnished yet natural light gold.

'What did you do?'

Luisa didn't recognise the woman in the mirror. A woman whose eyes looked larger, her face almost sculpted and quite…arresting. She turned her head, watching the slanting sunlight catch the seemingly artless fall of hair.

The Frenchwoman shrugged. 'A couple of highlights to accentuate your natural golden tones and a good cut. You approve?'

Luisa nodded, unable to find words to describe what she felt. She remembered those last months nursing her mother, poring with her over fashion and beauty magazines borrowed from the local library. Her mother, with her unerring eye for style, would point out the cut that would be perfect for Luisa. And Luisa would play along, pretending that when she'd finally made her choice she'd visit a salon and have her hair styled just so. As if she had time or money to spare for anything other than her mother's care and the constant demands of the farm.

'It's just long enough to put up for formal occasions.'

Luisa's stomach bottomed at the thought of the

formal occasions she'd face when they reached Maritz.

This couldn't be real. It couldn't be happening. *How could she have agreed?*

Suddenly she needed to escape. Needed to draw fresh air into her lungs, far from the confines of this gilt-edged mansion with its period furniture and discreet servants.

It hit her that, from the moment Raul had delivered his ultimatum, she'd not been alone. His security men had been on duty that final night she'd slept at home. Probably making sure she didn't do a midnight flit! After that there'd been stewards, butlers, chauffeurs.

And Raul himself, invading her personal space even when he stood as far from her as possible.

The stylist had barely slid the protective cape off Luisa's shoulders when she was on her feet, full of thanks for the marvellous cut and turning towards the door.

Her thoughts froze as the Frenchwoman looked at something over Luisa's shoulder then sank into a curtsey.

'Ah, Luisa, Mademoiselle. You've finished?' The deep voice curled across her senses like smoke on the air. She reminded herself it was distaste that made her shiver.

'Yes. We've finished.' Stiffening her spine, she turned.

Clear afternoon light spilled across the parquet floor and highlighted Raul where he stood just inside the doorway. Once again his splendour hit her full force. Not just the elegance of hand-stitched shoes and a beautifully crafted suit that clung to his broad shoulders. The impact of his strong personality was stamped on his austere features.

Even knowing his ruthlessness, it was hard not to gawk in appreciation. Luisa saw the stylist surreptitiously primping.

Annoyance sizzled. It wasn't just her. He had this effect on other women.

'I like your new look.' Raul's sudden smile was like warm honey. The flare of appreciation in his eyes even looked genuine. She told herself she didn't care.

'Thank you.' Her tone was stiff.

Yet Luisa's pulse raced. She put it down to dislike. How dared he come here with his gracious smile and his fluent French, charming her companion as if he were a kind benefactor!

Finally, after a long exchange of compliments, the stylist headed to the door. Luisa followed.

She should have known it wouldn't be so easy.

A firm hand grasped her elbow as she walked past Raul.

'Where are you going?'

'Out.' She looked pointedly at his restraining hand.

'That's impossible. You have another appointment.'

The simmering fury she'd battled for days spiked.

'Really? How strange. I don't recall making any appointment.' She raised her head, meeting his regard head-on. Letting her anger show.

Ever since she'd consented to go with him it had been the same. Exquisite politeness from him and deference from his staff. Yet every decision had been made for her.

At first she'd been in a state of shock, too stunned to do more than be swept along by the force of Raul's will. But her indignation had grown with each hour. Especially when she'd been told, not asked about appointments with the beautician, the pedicurist, the manicurist, the hair stylist, the couturier... As if she were an animated doll, not a woman with a brain of her own.

His hand dropped.

'You're upset.'

'You noticed!' She drew a slow breath, fighting

for control. She was rigid with outrage and self-disgust.

Luisa had spent enough time battling bullies. From her despotic grandfather to big banks eager for immediate returns. To this man who'd taken over her life.

She should have been able to stand up to him!
She'd never felt so helpless.

That scared her more than anything. And provoked her fighting spirit. She'd had enough!

'You're tired after the long journey.' Did his voice soften? Surely not.

She hadn't slept a wink, even in the luxurious bed assigned to her on the long haul flight to Europe. Yet fatigue was the least of her worries.

'I'm tired of you managing my life. Just because I gave in to blackmail doesn't mean I've relinquished the ability to think. I'm not a doormat.'

'No one would presume—'

'*You* presume all the time!' Luisa jabbed a finger into his broad chest then backed up a step, resolving to keep her distance. She didn't like the tiny pinprick of heat tickling her skin where she'd touched him. It was there too whenever he took her arm, helping her from a plane or car.

'You haven't once *asked*!' She spread her hands. 'Your staff simply tell me what you've decided.'

His hooded eyes gave nothing away, but the sharp angle of his jaw told her she'd hit home. Good! The idea of getting under this man's skin appealed. It was about time he found out what it felt like not to get his own way.

'Royalty works on a strict timetable.'

'And dairy farms don't?' She planted her hands on her hips. 'After you've spent your life getting up before dawn for early milking, *then* talk to me about managing my time!'

'It's hardly the same thing.'

'No, it's not.' She kept her voice calm with an effort. 'My life might not have been exciting but it was about honest hard work. A real job, doing something useful. Not—' she gestured to the exquisitely decorated salon and the man who stood so haughtily before her '—not empty gloss and privilege.'

A dull flush of colour streaked across Raul's razor-sharp cheekbones. Deep grooves bracketed the firm line of his mouth and his long fingers flexed and curled. Energy radiated from him, a latent power so tangible she had to force herself to stand her ground.

'You'll find royal life isn't a sinecure.' His words were glacial shards, grazing her overheated cheeks. 'Running a country is a demanding full-time job.'

Luisa refused to be cowed. Nothing excused his treatment of her. That had to change. Now.

'Under extreme duress I agreed to go to your country and accept my inheritance. That doesn't give you carte blanche to run my life.'

'Where were you going?' His question surprised her.

She glanced at the full length windows with their view of a wide, elegant boulevard and a distant park.

'I've never been to Paris.' She'd never travelled. Except to her grandfather's home and to Sydney when her mum visited specialists. Neither had been pleasant experiences. 'I want to explore.'

'You haven't time. Your new clothes are here and you need to be fitted. It's important you look like a princess when you step off the plane in Maritz.'

'In case I don't photograph well for the press?' She almost laughed at the idea of being media-worthy, but the way his face shuttered instantly at her mention of the press distracted her.

'It's for your sake as well, Luisa. Imagine arriving in the full blare of public interest, dressed as you are.'

Was that a hint of sympathy in his expression, or did she imagine it?

'There's nothing wrong with my clothes! They're...'

Cheap and comfortable and a little shabby. It wasn't that she didn't want beautiful clothes. It was the idea of pretending to be someone she wasn't, as if the real Luisa wasn't worth knowing. Yet a tiny voice inside admitted she didn't want to face a nation's press as she was.

She didn't want to face the press at all!

'Clothes are like armour.' His voice held a note of understanding that surprised her. 'You'll feel more comfortable in clothes that make you look good.'

Did he speak from personal experience? Seeing the proud tilt of his head, Luisa guessed Raul could walk naked before a crowd and not lose one ounce of his regal attitude.

Her breath hitched on the idea of Raul naked. With those long, powerful thighs and that rangy powerful torso...

With an effort she dragged her mind back on track.

'I don't need permission to go out.' She kept her voice low and even but her chin crept up. 'I don't answer to you and I *do* intend to see some of the city.'

She wouldn't let him dictate to her any more.

'Then what if I take you out myself, tonight?'

Luisa blinked in astonishment. 'I have appointments for the rest of the day but after dinner, if you like, I'll show you some of the sights of Paris.' He paused for a long moment, his mouth easing into what could almost pass for a smile. 'Would that suit?'

Blankly Luisa stared. A compromise? That must have cost him!

Instantly suspicion grew that he was up to something. Yet the idea of escaping this gorgeous, claustrophobic house was irresistible.

'Agreed.'

Six hours later Luisa stood against the railing of a river cruiser, straining forward as each new sight came into view. From the Ile de la Cité with Notre Dame's flying buttresses illuminated like spread wings against the darkness, to the Pont Neuf and the glittering Eiffel Tower. Paris slid around them, gorgeous and outrageously seductive. Yet still the tension twisted through her.

She and Raul were the only passengers.

Another reminder of what his wealth could buy.

Like her clothes. Stylish black wool trousers and a chic winter-weight cream tunic. Boots and a long coat of leather so soft she had to force herself not to keep smoothing her hands over it. A designer silk scarf in indigo and burnt orange that brought colour to her cheeks.

Except her cheeks burned anyway, remember-ing the designer's whispered asides to his assis-tant about Luisa's shape, size, posture and walk. Her posture was good, apparently, but her walk! A stride, like a man's. And she had no notion how to carry off a dress. None!

Yet, despite being an apparently insurmountable challenge, she'd been transformed.

Not that Raul had noticed. He'd escorted her to the car with barely a word. Luisa's bruised pride had been lacerated that he hadn't commented on her appearance. Clearly it was a matter of the utmost indifference to him.

And this the man who'd spoken of marriage!

She drew a slow breath. Once in Maritz she'd consult local lawyers. There must be a way out of the wedding contract. Fear scudded through her at the idea of marrying—

'You're enjoying yourself?' In the darkness she saw movement as Raul stood beside her. A trickle of heat warmed her belly and she swallowed hard. She hated the way her traitorous body responded yet she couldn't douse her excitement. Even in her teens, bowled over by what she thought was love, she hadn't felt this way.

'The city is beautiful. Thank you for the cruise.'

'So you admit there are benefits to our arrangement?'

His satisfied smile set her teeth on edge. He took credit for the beauty of the city, forgetting the blackmail that had forced her hand! It was a relief to let her frustration and indignation surge to the surface.

'They don't outweigh the negatives.'

He made an abrupt movement with one hand, a rare sign of impatience that surprised her. Usually he was so calm. 'You refuse to be pleased, no matter what you are offered.'

'I don't recall any *offer*. That implies choice.'

'You would rather be with your precious cows instead of here?' His wide gesture encompassed the magical vista. 'I give you the chance to be *queen*.'

'By *marrying* you!' She backed a step. 'I'll go with you to Maritz, but as for marriage...' Luisa shook her head.

The sharp glimmer of his stare triggered her innermost anxieties, releasing a tumble of words. 'You can't give me anything I truly desire!'

Years before a man had tried to take her, not out of passion, but calculating ambition. It had left her feeling unclean. That was when she'd decided she'd never settle for anything less than love.

'I want to marry a man who makes my heart race and my blood sing—'

Strong hands closed on her upper arms and she gaped up at the starkly sculpted face suddenly so close. A passing light played over him. Far from being coolly remote, heat ignited in Raul's eyes. His expression sent adrenalin surging.

His head lowered and his warm breath feathered her face.

'Like this, you mean?'

CHAPTER FOUR

Raul's mouth claimed Luisa's, pressing, demanding, till on a gasp her lips parted and he took possession.

Too late he realised his mistake.

The spark of indignation and guilt that had urged him to silence her grievances flared higher. Hotter. Brighter. He tasted her and heat shimmered, molten in his blood. He delved into her sweet, lush mouth and discovered something unexpected.

Something unique.

He slanted his mouth, demanding better access. Needing more. A ripple of stunned pleasure reverberated through him. He'd suspected almost from the start that there was something unique about Luisa. But this…!

His tongue slicked across hers, laved and slid and explored and there it was again.

An excitement, an anticipation he hadn't felt since he was a green boy.

Still it persisted. The feeling this was *different*.

He tugged her satisfyingly close between his

wide-planted legs. His other hand slid up into the thick silken mass of bright hair that had caught his eye as he'd walked into the salon this afternoon. He'd wanted to touch it ever since.

It felt even better than it looked, soft as seduction.

The fire dropped to his belly, kindling like a coiling Catherine wheel that jetted sparks in all directions.

Tension screwed unbearably tight as her hand fluttered at his throat, a barely there touch that weakened his knees. When she slid both arms over his shoulders to clasp his neck a great shudder rocked him.

How could a kiss ravage his senses?

Trying to staunch the feeling that he spun out of control, Raul moved his lips to the corner of her mouth but she turned her head. Instead of an almost chaste caress, he found himself transfixed as her lips opened beneath his. Her body pressed close and her tongue slipped into his mouth in a move that he'd have called tentative if it hadn't sent every blood cell in his body rushing south.

Her kiss was slow and deliberate. Unbelievably provocative as she treated him to a devastating sensual exploration that almost blew the top off his head. Shivers of delight coursed through him.

Once or twice she hesitated as if unsure how to

proceed. But the feel of her tongue mating with his in slow, lush pleasure soon obliterated such crazy notions.

Raul slid a hand under her long coat, over the tight curve of her bottom. His splayed fingers dragged her close, where that flicker of heat was now a blazing furnace. He tilted his pelvis and felt her welcoming feminine softness. Lust shot through him.

He swallowed her gasp, returning her kiss with growing fervour. Every nerve was sharp and aware, as if it had been an age since he'd held a woman.

Luisa tasted like sunshine, felt warm and soft and luscious like a summer peach.

Heat spiked in his groin and a hard weight surged there. The audacious notion rose that here, now, they should let passion take its inevitable course. He'd never felt such an unravelling of control.

Dimly he registered astonishment as desire blasted him. He met her kisses hungrily, her soft little whimper of pleasure driving him on even as he tried to slow down.

Luisa, with her sweet sensuality and her delicious hesitation, piqued an appetite jaded by over-eager women.

Brightness spilled over them, a wash of cold sanity.

Raul blinked in the light from an overhead bridge. He raised his head but his hands were still on her, their lower bodies welded together, even as they passed a group of sightseers peering down at the Seine.

Even now hunger gripped him.

Hell!

What was he doing, giving free rein to passion in public? It was unheard of! Raul kept his sex life scrupulously private after the nightmare scandal eight years ago. He'd worked tirelessly since to shore up his people's belief in and respect for the monarchy.

Yet he couldn't drag his eyes from Luisa, couldn't force himself to step away.

Her lips were parted. Her dark eyelashes fanned, concealing her eyes. She looked wantonly inviting and the heat in his groin intensified. His hold tightened.

Could this be the same woman he'd once thought unfeminine? She was beautiful.

Yet more was at work here than a no-expenses-spared makeover. Even if the result surpassed his expectations.

He met lovely women all the time. But none made him feel like this.

The women in his life were easy company, a pleasure to look at. They satisfied his need for sex.

He treated them well and they were eager to please. Simple. Uncomplicated.

Yet with Luisa he didn't merely respond to a pretty woman. Her fire, her determination, her strength made her unique. He *felt* as well as desired.

She stirred against him and a bolt of erotic energy speared him.

No! He imagined things. This desire was so intense because he'd allowed her to provoke anger.

He avoided dwelling on the fact that in itself was unusual. He'd learnt years before to channel all his energies into his work. Emotion had led him to the brink of disaster. The eventual fallout of that error had destroyed his family and threatened the state. Now he knew better. He controlled his world. Never again would he be a hostage to sentiment.

Luisa's eyes flickered open and a jewel-bright stare skewered him. His heart thudded out of kilter as his rationalisations crumbled.

Abruptly he released her and stepped away.

What had she done?

Heat blasted Luisa and she swayed, legs wobbling, as unfamiliar sensations cascaded through her.

She couldn't—surely she couldn't have kissed the man who'd *blackmailed* her into doing his bidding?

Surely she hadn't...*enjoyed* it?

Cool air chilled her face and crept in the open front of her jacket. Yet she burned up, her cheeks fiery. Heat seared through her stomach and down to the terrible hollow throb between her legs.

Inwardly she cringed. So much for defiance. And for self-respect. What had happened to the reserve that had kept her impervious to the masculine sex for so long? The wariness borne of disillusionment and hurt?

Raul had hauled her into his embrace, kissed her and her brain had shorted. She'd gone from indignation to helpless need, craving each demanding caress.

How could she have responded to a man she surely hated?

And to have revealed her inexperience to him! No way could her shaming enthusiasm have made up for her lack of expertise. He knew now just how naïve she was. How he must be smirking. The country bumpkin, easy to twist around his little finger. Show her a taste of what she'd never had and she'd be eating out of his hand.

Sickening echoes of the past filled her brain. Hadn't she learned? How could she be susceptible again? Self-disgust was bitter on her tongue.

Reluctantly she opened her eyes.

Instantly he moved away, his brows drawing down in a ferocious scowl as if he couldn't believe he'd touched her.

Pain speared her. No doubt she didn't measure up to his exacting royal standards. Déjà vu swamped her, recalling the scathing revelations of her long-ago suitor.

'I don't want you touching me.' Her voice was raw, husky with distress.

Raul loomed taller, his frown morphing in an instant to a look of cool composure.

'That wasn't the impression you gave a moment ago.' He tugged at his shirt, straightened his jacket, and Luisa felt about an inch tall, realising she'd pulled his clothing askew.

'I didn't invite you to maul me.' Conveniently she ignored the way she'd given herself up to his kiss. Even now she held onto the railing to stay upright. He turned her bones to water.

In the dimming light as the boat slid away from the bridge, it looked like colour rose in his cheeks. But that had to be her imagination. His expression grew haughty and his eyes glittered.

'My apologies. You can be sure I don't make a habit of *forcing my attentions* where they're not wanted.'

Raul drew himself up like a guard on parade.

Then with a flourish of one elegant hand he bowed formally. 'I'll leave you to your contemplation of the view.'

He turned and strode to the wheelhouse. He looked utterly calm, as if their passion had been a figment of her imagination. As if he'd felt nothing.

Surely not! He'd been as hungry for her as she'd been for him.

Or had he? She bit her lip, all too aware she had next to no experience to draw upon and that her judgement of men was flawed. Years ago she'd been dumbfounded when her ardent suitor finally revealed his true self when thwarted. His disdainful dismissal of her attractiveness and lack of sophistication was still vivid.

The possibility that Raul too had feigned desire made her want to sink through the deck.

Why should he do it?

The answer came too readily. To reduce her to starry-eyed compliance.

Luisa sagged against the railing.

It had worked. When he kissed her all her doubts and anger fled. She was putty in his hands. His kisses had been white-hot lightning, blowing her mind and leaving her body humming with a desperate craving.

She stared at his tall form as he disappeared

into the darkness. Vivid as her recall was of that near seduction years ago, Luisa couldn't remember kisses as devastating as this. Was her memory faulty? Or had years focused on work and family, shying from any tentative male interest, made her more susceptible?

The trembling in her knees grew to a quaking that shook her whole body.

Her impossible position had just become impossibly complicated.

Raul thrust aside a surge of regret as Luisa emerged from her suite. It was unfortunate he'd had to force her hand. Her vulnerability and her desperate pride struck a chord with him. And her passion—

No! Last night was over. A passing weakness.

He was in control now. Impossible that his feelings were engaged by the woman at the top of the staircase. He didn't do feelings. Not any more. One disastrous mistake had cured him.

Though in her chic honey-gold trouser suit and black silk shirt, Luisa was eye-catching. The suit skimmed ripe curves he'd held just hours ago. His fingers flexed at the memories, still vivid after a night of no rest.

She cast a flickering half glance in his direction and chewed on her glossy lower lip.

A ripple of something urgent disturbed his inner calm.

Stoically he ignored it, focusing an appraising eye on how she descended the grand staircase. She gripped the banister tight, clearly unsure of herself in high heels.

As he'd suspected. She'd need help when they arrived in Maritz in a few hours. He didn't want her falling down the steps from the plane and breaking her neck.

His gaze lingered on the long line of her throat. She had a natural elegance her farm clothes had camouflaged. His hands tingled as he recalled the feel of her soft skin, the temptation of her lips, the way her eyes flashed when she challenged him.

Her gaze snared his and his pulse slowed to a weighted thud.

Raul frowned. It was one thing to feel desire with a warm woman pressed intimately against him in the night. Quite another to experience it here, with his butler waiting to usher them on their way to the airport.

Worse, this felt more complex than lust. In a couple of short days she'd somehow got into his head.

Instantly he rejected the idea. It was simple desire he experienced.

'Luisa. I hope you slept well.'

He walked forward as she reached the bottom step. She stumbled and his hand shot out to steady her, but she jerked her arm away, hurrying past him, heels clicking on inlaid marble.

Raul drew a sharp breath. After a lifetime fending off eager women he discovered he didn't like this alternative.

He recalled how she'd clung so needily last night and assured himself her response was contrived. Women were devious. Was it any wonder he kept relationships simple?

What sort of relationship would he have with his wife?

'Yes, thank you. I slept well enough.'

Liar! Despite the make-up accentuating the smoky blue of her eyes, Raul saw signs of fatigue.

'And you?' To his surprise challenge sizzled in her gaze, as if she knew he'd spent most of the night wakeful, reliving those few moments when she'd melted into him like a born seductress.

Even now he wasn't sure about her. There'd been more than a hint of the innocent about her last night.

But then feigned innocence could be such an effective weapon. As he knew to his cost. A spike of chill air stabbed the back of his neck.

'I always sleep well in Paris.' He offered his arm again, this time holding her gaze till she complied.

He covered her hand with his, securing it possessively. The sooner she grew accustomed to him the better. 'And now, if you're ready, our plane is waiting.'

He felt the shiver race through her. Saw her eyes widen in what looked like anxiety.

There was nothing to fear. Most women would sell their soul to be in her place, offered wealth, prestige and marriage to a man the press insisted on labelling one of the world's most eligible bachelors. But already he began to see Luisa wasn't most women.

He heard himself saying, 'I'll look after you, Luisa. There's no need to be anxious.'

It was on the way to the airport that Raul discovered the cost of his unguarded actions last night. The discreet buzz of his mobile phone and a short conversation with Lukas, already waiting for them at the airport, had him excusing himself and opening his laptop.

Not that Luisa noticed. She was busy pressing her nose to the glass as they drove through Paris.

He focused on his computer, scrolling through

page after page of newspaper reports. The sort of reports he habitually ignored: 'PRINCE'S SECRET LOVER.' 'RAUL'S PARISIAN INTERLUDE.' 'SIZZLING SEDUCTION ON THE SEINE.'

There wasn't much to the articles apart from speculation as to his new lover's identity. Yet acid curdled his stomach and clammy heat rose as he flicked from one photo of last night's kiss to another.

He frowned, perplexed by his reaction.

It wasn't the first time the paparazzi had snapped photos of him with a woman. He was a favourite subject. Typically the press was more interested in his mistresses than his modernisation plans or regional disarmament talks. Usually he shrugged off their reports.

But this time…

Understanding dawned on a wave of nausea.

This time the photographer had unwittingly caught him in a moment of rare vulnerability. The press couldn't know, but Raul had been careening out of control, swept away by dangerously unfamiliar forces. Prey to a compulsion he hadn't experienced in years.

Eight years in fact.

Since the feeding frenzy of press speculation

about a royal love triangle. The memory sickened him.

Since he'd learned to distrust female protestations of love and displays of innocence. Since he'd rebuilt his shattered world with determination, pride and a complete absence of emotion that made a man vulnerable.

His gut cramped as he remembered facing the press, made rabid by the scent of blood—*his* blood. The effort of appearing unmoved in the face of the ultimate betrayal. Of how he'd had to claw back his self-respect after making the worst mistake of his life. How day after day he'd had to appear strong. Till finally the façade had become reality and he'd learned to live without emotional ties. Except for his love of Maritz.

He shut the laptop with a snap.

The cases weren't the same. Then he'd been naïve enough to believe in romance. He'd hurt with the intensity of youthful emotions. Now, at thirty, Raul was in control of his world. What he'd felt last night had been lust, more intense than usual perhaps, but simple enough.

Besides, public interest in Luisa could be used to advantage. It wouldn't hurt to hint that there was more to his approaching nuptials than fulfilment of a legal contract. People liked to believe in fairy tales and it would ease the way for her.

A lost princess, a romantic interlude in Paris, an early wedding. It was the sort of PR that would focus interest on the monarchy and dampen the enthusiasm for political rabble-rousing in the lead up to his coronation.

He'd planned a quiet arrival in Maritz to give Luisa time to acclimatise. Yet in the circumstances revealing her identity had definite benefits.

He'd arrange it with Lukas at the airport.

'You can unfasten your seat belt, ma'am.' The hostess smiled at Luisa on her way to open the plane door.

Foreboding lurched in the pit of Luisa's stomach.

The idea of stepping out of the aircraft and into the country that had once been her mother's, and her detested grandfather's, terrified her. Some atavistic foreknowledge warned that this next step would be irrevocable.

Again she experienced that sense of the world telescoping in around her, shrinking to a dark tunnel where her future lay immutable before her.

Desperately she sought for something positive to hang onto. The determination to get legal advice on that marriage contract as soon as she could. To find an escape clause that would allow Raul to inherit the throne he coveted without marrying her.

'Here.' A deep voice cut through her swirling thoughts. 'Let me.' Warm hands, large and capable, unclipped the seat belt and brushed it off her lap.

Sensation jittered through her stomach and across her thighs. Luisa looked up sharply to find Raul bending over her, his eyes warm with an expression she couldn't fathom.

Her heart rose in her throat, pounding fast. The memory of last night's madness filled her. The feel of his tight embrace and her need for more. Despite today's polite formality, nothing could obliterate the recollection. Even the knowledge it had been a lie. He'd felt nothing.

He stepped back and she sucked in an uneven breath.

'It's time to go.' He extended an arm.

Luisa nodded, her tongue glued to the roof of her mouth. What was happening to her? She had no desire to fall into Raul's arms again, yet she imagined warmth in his gaze. When all he cared about was her usefulness to him.

Silently she let him drape a cashmere coat over her shoulders, then stepped to the door. The sooner she reached their destination, the sooner she could sort out this mess.

A roar filled her ears and she stopped abruptly at the head of the stairs. She blinked into the bright light, wishing she'd brought sunglasses.

'It's all right,' Raul said. 'They're just glad to see us.'

He slid an arm slid round her, drawing her to him. Instinctively she pulled away but his hold was unbreakable.

'Relax,' he murmured. 'I'm just making sure you don't trip on those high heels. Come on.'

At his urging they descended, Luisa clinging to the railing and inordinately grateful for his support. Sheer bravado had led her to wear the highest heels in her new wardrobe, determined to look as sophisticated as possible. The move had backfired when she'd come face to face with Raul and discovered the extra height merely brought her closer to his knowing gaze.

Another roar made her blink and focus on the scene ahead.

Crowds massed behind the fence at the edge of the tarmac. Maritzian flags waved and excited voices called out. Luisa's Maritzian was rusty so all she could make out was Raul's name. *And hers.*

She stumbled to a stop on the narrow stairs and only Raul's firm grip saved her. Adrenalin pumped hard in her blood. From the near fall or perhaps from the impact of meeting his intent scrutiny head-on.

'What's happening?'

He shrugged and she felt the movement against her as he kept a tight hold of her waist.

'Well-wishers. Nothing to worry about.'

Luisa frowned, battling a rising sense of unreality. 'But how do they know my name?'

Something flickered in his eyes. 'Your identity isn't a secret. Is it?'

Dazedly she shook her head, beginning her descent again at his urging. 'But it makes no sense. How could—'

The sight of a placard in the throng cut off the words mid-flow. It showed her name and Raul's, linked in a massive love heart topped with a crown.

She swung round and read satisfaction in his face.

'What have you done?' Every muscle tightened as she fought the impulse to run back up the steps and hide in the royal jet.

His brows arched. 'I authorised my staff to confirm your identity if queried. Now, it's time we moved.'

Mutinously Luisa stared up at him, her hand tightening on the rail.

His eyes flashed, then his lips tilted in a one-sided smile that obliterated the grimness engraved around his lips, making him look younger. 'As you wish, madam.'

He bowed. But it wasn't a bow, she realised as his arms circled her.

Seconds later he hefted her up against his chest. The noise of the crowd crested in a swell of approval. But Luisa barely heard it over the thunderous beat of blood in her ears.

She should hate being manhandled. She did! Almost.

'What are you doing?' she demanded, trying not to focus on the feel of tough muscle and bone surrounding her.

His smile deepened and something flipped over inside Luisa's chest. He shrugged again and this time the movement rippled around her, drawing her closer.

It scared her how much she enjoyed being held by Raul.

'Carrying my bride down the stairs.'

CHAPTER FIVE

LUISA walked across the tarmac towards the crowd. It was daunting. So huge, so excited. For an insane moment she wished she were back in his arms. To her consternation she'd felt…safe there.

Her knees shook with every step. His arm around her waist was both a torment and a support.

She swallowed hard, nervous at what she faced. And furious.

'Don't faint on me now, Luisa.'

'No chance of that,' she managed through gritted teeth as instinctively she tried to respond to the broad smiles on so many faces. 'I'm not going to swoon in your arms. Even for the sake of your audience.'

'*Our* audience.'

A barrage of flashes set up around them. He raised one hand in acknowledgement and the crowd cheered harder.

The information she'd found on the web mentioned his dedication to his country but she hadn't realised how popular he was. Cynically she did a quick survey of the crowd and noticed women out-numbered men three to one. That explained some of the excitement.

It would be easy to fall for Raul if you didn't know the man behind the gorgeous exterior.

He swept her towards a gleaming limousine. No lengthy wait for passport and customs checks for him.

They'd almost reached the car when Luisa saw what had provoked such interest. Someone held up a page from a newspaper, with a blown up photo of a couple embracing so passionately it felt voyeuristic to look at them.

It took a moment for the truth to slam into her. The man staring so intently down at the woman he held possessively was Raul. His face was harsh with stark sexual hunger. Or intense calculation.

And the woman with her kiss-swollen lips, apparently swooning in his arms, was her!

Luisa's skin crawled in horror. Bile rose in her throat and she swallowed frantically. She felt… violated at the knowledge anyone else had seen that moment. Had viewed her vulnerability. Bad enough Raul knew her appalling weakness, but to have others witness it, splash it in newsprint…

She gasped, her breath sawing painfully in cramped lungs.

'Come, Luisa.' Raul urged her forwards. 'Don't stop here in front of the cameras.'

The mention of cameras moved her on till she found herself seated, shivering, in a limo. Her brain seemed to have seized up and her teeth were chattering.

'Luisa?' Warm hands chafed her icy ones. Dazedly she heard a muttered imprecation, then her knees were swathed in warmth as Raul tucked his jacket around her legs.

'I don't need it. I'm fine.' Her voice sounded over-loud in the thick silence now the privacy screen had been raised. But a chance glance out of the window to the people milling about, watching their vehicle, made her shrink back into the soft leather.

'You've had a shock. I apologise. I should have warned you.' Luisa could almost believe that was genuine regret in his deep voice.

But her brain was branded with the memory of his expression in that photo. She wasn't stupid enough to believe he'd been overcome by passion. He'd recovered too fast and too completely. He'd probably been calculating how successful his seduction had been. Assessing how compliant she'd be in future.

Fury pierced the fog of shock.

'*You* did that!' She rounded on him, too angry to

feel more than a tremor of surprise at how close he sat, his thigh warm against hers. 'You set me up for that photo.' How could she have forgotten her suspicion last night when he'd suggested taking her out? She should have guessed he was up to something.

Hauteur iced his features.

'I don't do deals with the paparazzi.'

Luisa shook her head. 'Someone did! They were there, waiting for us. You can't tell me—'

'I *do* tell you, Luisa.' His voice held a note of steel that silenced her. 'I have nothing but contempt for the media outlets and the photographers who spend their time beating up such stories.' His jaw tightened and Luisa found herself sinking back into her seat.

Gullible she might be, but everything from the set of his taut shoulders to the glitter in his dark eyes convinced her he was telling the truth.

'The press are always on the watch for photo opportunities. They follow constantly, though given my security detail, usually at a distance. It's part of being royal. A fact of life.'

'I don't think much of being royal then.' Her stomach was painfully tight after the sudden welling nausea.

To her surprise, Raul's mouth lifted in a rare

smile that made something inside her soften. 'I don't either. Not that part of it.'

His hand enfolded hers and for an instant she knew a bizarre urge to smile back, sharing a moment of intimacy.

Except it was a mirage. There *was* no intimacy.

'I regret the photo, Luisa. If I'd realised we were visible...' He shrugged.

To her amazement she found herself wanting to believe him. 'But even if the press had reported our—' she swallowed, her mouth dry as she remembered his kiss '—our trip on the river, I don't see why the crowd would be excited about my arrival. Surely they don't turn out to see all your... girlfriends.'

His smile faded and his grip tightened. Clearly he didn't like explaining himself.

Tough!

Luisa dragged her hand from his, refusing to notice the loss of warmth.

'I told you. I instructed my staff to explain who you are if asked.'

'But my name wouldn't mean anything!'

Silently he surveyed her as if waiting for her to catch up. 'Your title does. Princess Luisa of Ardissia.'

Luisa froze as the implications sank in. 'I'm not princess yet. I haven't signed—'

'But you will.' His voice was a rich, creamy purr. 'That's why you came, isn't it?'

She nodded, feeling again that hated sense of being cornered. Suspicion flared.

'That's not all they said, is it?' Urgently she leaned towards him, thrusting his jacket off her legs, uncaring she was close enough to see the individual long lashes fringing his eyes, or the hint of a nick on his smoothly shaven jaw. To inhale the warm scent of his skin.

'They just happened to mention the marriage contract, didn't they?'

Raul held her gaze unblinkingly and for one crazy moment she felt an echo of last night's emotions when he'd hauled her close and introduced her to bliss.

Heat scorched her cheeks and throat.

'Didn't they?'

'It's not a secret, Luisa, though the details weren't widely known.'

She sat back, her heart pounding.

'You don't give up, do you?' It shouldn't come as a surprise. Not after he'd manoeuvred her into coming here. 'What did you hope to achieve? Pressure me into agreeing?'

It was as if he'd known she still held out hope of avoiding marriage. Wearily she raised a hand to her forehead, smoothing the beginning of an ache there.

'I won't be forced into marriage because your precious public expects it. If I pull out the story would be all about you. How you were jilted. Not about me.'

In an instant his face whitened to the colour of scoured bone. His nostrils flared and the flesh seemed to draw back, leaving his clear cut features spare and prominent. Almost she could believe she'd scored some unseen injury.

Energy radiated from him. A sense of barely controlled power. Of danger.

This time she did retreat.

'There will be no jilting.' Fascinated, Luisa saw the tic of Raul's pulse at his jaw.

'I will not leave my people to the chaos that would come if I gave up the throne.' He paused. 'Remember why you agreed to come here.'

Blazing eyes meshed with hers and any hope she'd harboured that he wouldn't follow through on his threat vanished. This man would do whatever it took to get what he wanted. How had she let last night's fake tenderness blind her to that? Or his solicitude here in the car?

Luisa pulled her jacket close and turned to face the window. She couldn't face him with her emotions so raw.

They'd left the highway for the old part of the city. Cobblestones rumbled under the wheels as they crossed a wide square of pastel-coloured baroque buildings that housed expensive shops.

The car turned and before them appeared a steep incline, almost a cliff. Above that, seeming to grow from the living rock, towered the royal castle. Dark grey stone with round towers and forest green roofs just visible behind the massive battlement.

Guidebooks said the castle was a superb example of medieval construction, updated with spectacular eighteenth century salons and modern amenities. That it commanded extraordinary views to the Alps and down the wide river valley. That its treasure house was unrivalled in central Europe and its ballroom an architectural gem.

But what stuck in Luisa's mind was that in almost a millennium of use no one had ever escaped the castle's dungeons once locked up by order of the king.

Her suite of rooms was airy, light and sumptuous. Not at all like a dank prison cell. Yet Luisa barely took in the silk and gilt loveliness.

She stood before the wide windows, staring to distant snow-capped mountains. That was where Ardissia lay. The place that tied her to wealth and position and a life of empty gloss instead of emotional warmth and security. Tied her to Raul. A man whose ambition repelled, yet who made her tremble with glorious, dreadful excitement.

Luisa trailed her fingers appreciatively over the antique desk. It wasn't that she didn't like beautiful things, or the designer clothes wealth could buy. It was that she knew they weren't any substitute for happiness. For warmth and caring and love. She'd grown up with love and her one disastrous foray into romance had taught her she couldn't accept anything else.

On impulse she snatched up the phone. A dialling tone buzzed in her ear and her heart leapt at the idea of calling home. She looked at her watch, calculating the time difference. With the help of the phone book she found the international code and rang home.

'Oh, pet! It's so good to hear your voice.' Mary's excited chatter eased some of the tension drawn tight in Luisa's stomach. She sank back onto a silk upholstered chair in front of the desk.

'We've been wondering how you are and what you're doing. Are you well? How was the trip? Did that lovely Prince Raul look after you?'

Luisa bit her lip at the memory of how well Raul had looked after her. He'd played on her vulnerability and used his own compelling attraction to lay bare naïve longings she hadn't even realised she harboured.

'The trip was fine, Mary. I even had my own bed on the plane. And then we stopped in Paris—'

'Paris? Really?'

Soon Luisa was swept along by Mary's demands for details, peppered with her aunt's exclamations and observations. Eventually the talk turned to home.

'We've been missing you, love. It seems strange with that new bloke and his son in your house. But I can't deny they've made a good start. He's a decent manager, by the look of it. And he reckons the changes you and your dad began to modernise the co-op were spot on. Well, I could have told him that! And between you and me, it's such a relief knowing that debt's going to be settled. Sam is like a new man without that weighing on him. And Josie's all agog about moving into town to take up an apprenticeship, now we'll be able to afford to help her with rent. And little Julia Todd is looking so much better these days. I was worried about her being so wan. It turns out the poor thing is pregnant again and was worried about how they'd afford another child. But now she's positively radiant...'

Luisa leaned forward to put her elbow on the desk, letting her head sink onto her hand.

Mary's voice tugged at something deep inside. The part of her that longed for everything familiar and dear.

Yet with each new breathless revelation it became clear Luisa couldn't go back. Her past, the life she'd loved, were closed to her.

The last vestige of hope had been torn away today when she looked into fathomless emerald eyes and a stern, beautiful face. Raul would do whatever it took to get the crown he coveted.

Already the people she loved were moving on, anticipating the cancellation of the co-op's debts. Luisa had understood that, but not till this moment had the devastating reality of it all hit her fully.

Luisa had no choice.

She lifted her head and looked around the delicately lovely room. *A room for a princess.*

She shuddered at the enormity of what faced her.

But her parents' example was vivid in her mind. No matter what life threw at them, they'd battled on, making the most of life without complaint.

Luisa set her jaw. It was time she faced her future.

* * *

'Raul.'

He looked up from the papers he and Lukas were discussing—disturbing reports of more unrest.

Luisa stood in the doorway. A dart of heat shot through him as he took in her loveliness and re-membered the taste of her lips beneath his.

There was something different about her. Gone was the distressed woman of mere hours ago. And the woman endearingly unsure of herself in high heels. This was Luisa as he'd first seen her—confi-dent and in control, yet with no hint of the farmyard about her.

She looked…magnificent.

He shoved back his chair and stood. 'We'll con-tinue later, Lukas.' His assistant hastily packed up the reports and bowed himself from the study, clos-ing the door.

'Please take a seat.'

She crossed the room to halt before his desk. 'This won't take long.' She paused, her slightly stunned gaze taking in his state-of-the-art com-puter equipment and the large document storage area behind him. As if surprised to discover he actually worked.

Raul paced around the desk. 'What can I do for you, Luisa?' It was the first time she'd sought him out.

Clear blue eyes met his and he felt that now-familiar frisson of anticipation.

'I've come to tell you I'll do it. I'll marry you.'

Raul breathed deep as the knot of tension that had screwed his belly tight for so long loosened.

He'd manipulated her into coming here. He'd overseen a new look for her, introduced her to his people in such a way she'd be cornered by their expectations, and still he hadn't been sure he could go through with it. Force her into marriage.

Despite his determination and his desperation, doubts had preyed on him.

'What made you change your mind?'

She shrugged. 'Does it matter?'

Raul opened his mouth. Part of him believed it did. The part that wanted to know Luisa better, her thoughts and feelings. The part of him, he supposed, that had made him emotionally susceptible all those years ago. The part he'd thought he'd erased from his being.

He shook his head. What mattered was her agreement.

'I thought not.' Her eyes blazed with what might have been anger. Then, in a moment, the look was gone.

He took her hand in his. She didn't resist.

'I promise you, Luisa, I will do everything in my

power to ensure you never regret this.' His skin grew tight over tense muscles as he thought of the enormity of her decision. Of all it meant for him and his people.

He lifted her hand to his lips.

'You will have my gratitude and my loyalty.' Her flesh was cool, her expression shuttered and yet he felt the trembling pulse at her wrist. He inhaled her delicate scent. Something far stronger than gratitude stirred in his belly.

'You owe me more.'

Startled, he raised his head. She slipped her hand free and clasped it in her other palm as if it pained her.

'What do you want?'

She'd almost convinced him she didn't care for wealth and glamour. Now suspicion rose. He should have known better. Hadn't Ana taught him anything? What was her price?

'I want...' She paused and gestured abruptly with one hand. 'I *don't* want to be treated as some brainless doll. As far as possible, I want to make my own decisions. Don't expect to dictate to me.'

Raul took in the defiant glimmer in her eyes, the determined jut of her chin and felt the tension leach away.

No unreasonable demands? No tantrums or tears?

Pride stirred, and respect for this remarkable woman.

Perhaps after all Luisa was as unique as she seemed.

His lips curved in a smile of genuine pleasure. 'I wouldn't expect anything less.'

Raul saw Luisa led past the royal councillors, across the vast reception room. The soon-to-be-Princess of Ardissia was quietly elegant in shades of caramel and cream. Her back was straight and her chin up as if unfazed by the presence of so many august people. Yet she was pale and there was a brittle quality to her composure that made his brow knot.

Guilt pinched. A few days ago she'd been leading a completely different life. Had he been right to move so fast to cement this arrangement?

Raul stiffened, refusing to follow that line of thought. This was for the best. For the good of the nation. The alternative would plunge the country into chaos.

The sooner this was done the better.

He strode across the room, silently berating himself for getting sidetracked by urgent negotiations. He'd meant to support her as she entered the room.

He'd nearly reached her at the ornate desk when

she saw him and started. Disappointment flared. This wasn't the first time she'd reacted as if his touch contaminated.

It took a moment to realise that in flinging out an arm involuntarily Luisa had knocked over the baccarat crystal inkwell. Black liquid sprayed across the hand woven heirloom carpet and his suit.

The room inhaled a collective gasp. In a moment Luisa had ripped blotting paper from the embossed blotter on the desk and dropped to her knees, soaking up the stain.

Servants rushed to assist but she didn't notice. 'We need something to soak this up.'

Raul dragged a pristine handkerchief from his pocket and hunkered beside her. 'Will this help?'

'Not much.' Her words were crisp. 'But it's better than nothing.' The snowy cloth joined the dark pulpy mass on the carpet.

'Excuse me, ma'am. Ma'am?' One of the senior staff appeared with materials to clear the worst of the mess.

'Luisa.' Raul took her elbow, gripping tight enough to make her look up. 'The staff will deal with this.'

She opened her mouth as if to protest, then looked over his shoulder, eyes widening. As if she'd only just remembered every member of the High Court, the royal advisors and sundry VIPs here to witness the formalities.

Heat flooded her face and she looked away. Gently he drew her to her feet.

She felt surprisingly fragile beneath his touch. Not like the woman who'd seduced him witless with just a kiss, or the proud woman who'd agreed to marry him.

'I'm sorry.' She watched the staff deal with a stain that was probably immovable, worrying at her lower lip.

'It's all right,' he murmured, leading her away to the other side of the desk.

'But the carpet! It's old and valuable, surely?' Her hands clenched tight.

'No such thing. It's amazing how well they make reproductions these days.'

He heard his butler's breath hiss at the blithe lie. In Raul's father's day, damaging an heirloom like this would have resulted in severe punishment. But, seeing Luisa's distress, feeling her arm tremble beneath his hold, Raul didn't give a damn about anything but allaying her guilt.

'Come,' he said. 'Here's a seat for you.'

She sank into the chair and Raul swept the blotter aside, motioning for the accession document to be brought forward. Reaching in his jacket, he withdrew his own pen.

Maritz needed to move with the times. There was absolutely no need to continue the tradition of signing and witnessing important documents with old-fashioned ink pens.

Lukas presented the document which, when signed, would confirm Luisa as Princess of Ardissia, inheritor of her grandfather's wealth. And Raul's wife-to-be.

It was spread wide on the desk and the witnesses stepped forward. Raul handed her the pen.

And waited.

For Luisa didn't sign. Instead, she read the English translation, slowly and methodically. Her finger marked a difficult clause and she lifted her head, turning to Lukas who hovered helpfully on her other side.

'Would you mind explaining this reference?' she murmured softly.

'Of course, ma'am.' After a quick look at Raul, Lukas bent over the parchment, explaining the clause. Then after a few moments, another.

The audience grew restless. Raul noticed one or two raised brows among some of the more old-fashioned advisers. He could imagine what they whispered. That the woman should gratefully accept what was offered, without question.

Luisa was aware of the buzz of comment. Her cheeks grew brighter and he saw her neck stiffen. Yet still she read each line.

It should have annoyed him, this delay to his plans. Even now, on the edge of achieving what was so necessary, ripples of anxiety spread through his belly. He couldn't be completely happy till this was settled.

Yet his impatience was tempered by admiration. Luisa was naturally cautious.

Like him. He'd never sign anything without careful consideration either.

Raul recalled the advice he'd recently received. That on investigation Luisa's farming co-op was found to be surprisingly well run. That the financial difficulties were due to the economic downturn, a massive drought and a series of unfortunate health problems, including the death of her father last year.

According to the accountants, the business was poised to become very successful, once money was freed up for new equipment. Luisa had done an excellent job.

Once more curiosity rose. She wasn't like other women. He'd been so intent on achieving his ends he'd initially thought of her as a convenient bride, not a real woman. Now he pondered exactly what sort of woman he would wed.

He looked at her bent head, how she bit her lush bottom lip in concentration. Fire arced through his gut.

She fascinated him, he admitted now. Her obstinacy, pragmatism and quiet pride. Her unassuming ways and her disquieting sensuality. *How long since a woman had intrigued him so? Since a kiss had made him lose his head?*

Finally, with a swift movement, Luisa picked up his pen and signed. Only Raul, close beside her, saw the way her hand shook. It pained him to see what this cost her.

Yet relief swamped him. It was almost done. Soon the crown would be his. His destiny was within his grasp. His country would be safe.

He picked up the pen, still warm from her fingers, and with a flourish added his signature as first witness. 'Thank you, Luisa,' he murmured.

At his words she tilted her head and their gazes meshed. Heat ricocheted through his belly and groin, the reverberations spreading even as she looked away, letting her lashes veil her eyes.

Now she was bound to him, this intriguing woman so lacking in sophistication yet with an innate grace and integrity he couldn't ignore.

Theirs would be a convenient marriage. A marriage of state for the well-being of the nation.

Yet, to his astonishment, Raul registered a purely personal satisfaction at the prospect.

CHAPTER SIX

'I COULDN'T have done a better job of botching that if I'd tried.' Luisa grimaced as she followed Lukas through a maze of corridors to her suite.

She'd do better in future.

Her skin crawled at the memory of censorious eyes on her: an upstart foreigner, not only gauche but clumsy.

'Nothing of the sort, ma'am. You carried it off with great composure.'

Luisa smiled gratefully. Lukas really was a nice man. Surprisingly nice for someone in the Prince's employ.

'Thanks, Lukas, but there's no need to pretend. I saw the way they looked, and their impatience that I wanted to read what I signed.'

'It's true some of the advisers are rather old school.' Lukas cleared his throat and gestured for her to precede him down another wide corridor. 'I'm sure His Highness wouldn't mind me saying that's been one of his challenges in running the country as a modern state—bringing them along in the process of reform.'

Luisa's eyes widened. It hadn't occurred to her Raul would have difficulties. With his take charge attitude and formidable determination she couldn't imagine it.

'You talk as if he's been in charge of the country a long time. I thought the King only died recently.'

A hint of a flush coloured Lukas' cheeks. 'That's correct, ma'am.' He paused and then, with the air of making a sudden decision, added, 'But His Highness was in many ways responsible for running the country long before that. The previous king…left a lot in the Prince's hands.'

Luisa's mind snagged on Lukas' words, trying to read the subtext. There was one. Something he skated around rather than spelling out. It was on the tip of her tongue to press for an explanation, till she read his discomfort.

'And is it still difficult?'

Lukas shrugged. 'The Prince has made his mark and even the more old-fashioned courtiers see the benefits. But there are some who resent change. Some who'd rather vie for personal power than cooperate in a national effort to modernise.'

Her steps slowed. Lukas' assessment echoed Raul's words. She'd half dismissed that as a smokescreen, veiling the fact he simply coveted the crown. Though lately she'd wondered. Seeing him with others, she'd caught glimpses of a reasonable man, even a caring one.

Was there more truth in Raul's words than she'd thought? He claimed he acted for the country as well as himself. Was it possible? It was tempting to hope so.

Yet nothing excused Raul's behaviour towards her.

'As for today, ma'am,' Lukas said, 'I know the Prince was very pleased with your first official appearance.'

She just bet he was! She'd signed his precious documents. Yet she hadn't missed the way he'd hovered, eager for her to sign and be done with it. If she was truthful, it wasn't just the habit of reading legal papers carefully that had made her delay. A tiny part of her had wanted him on tenterhooks, wondering if she'd go through with it.

As if she'd had a choice! Besides, she'd given her word.

Her heart plunged at the implications of what she'd just done. No turning back now.

'Lukas, I've changed my mind. Can you show me the way to the gardens? I need some fresh air.'

* * *

Forty minutes later Luisa felt less claustrophobic. Wandering through the courtyards she'd found a gardener. They'd discussed the grounds with enthusiasm and sign language since her Maritzian was sparse and Gregor, the gardener, spoke a particularly thick dialect.

They'd toured the terraces and rose garden, where Luisa recognised the names of gorgeous old roses her mother had mentioned. They'd visited an orchard in the moat, a walled garden with fountains and arbours and the kitchen garden where Luisa struggled to identify the rarer herbs.

For the first time in days she felt as if she'd stepped out of her nightmare and into the real world, with the scent of rich soil and growing things around her.

She breathed deep as she climbed the spiral staircase in the battlements. Gregor had said, if she understood right, that she'd see the parterre garden from here. She'd read about such gardens, with their intricate patterns laid out in plants and gravel paths, but the view from the ground didn't give the full effect.

She could have seen it from the castle. But she didn't want to meet any of the disapproving VIPs who'd witnessed her accession to the title of Princess of Ardissia.

Princess! Her stomach curdled, thinking about it.

Or was that because of the tower? She didn't have a head for heights and the open window beside her gave a dizzying view to the city below.

Luisa pressed a damp palm to the wall and kept moving. Soon she emerged at a low opening looking towards the castle. Someone had been working here and she side-stepped a pile of tools. The opening was so low she felt safer on her knees, her hands on the stonework.

The garden was spectacular, though overgrown. She made out the remnants of the Maritzian dragon, the one flying on the flag from the topmost turret, laid out in the hedges below. Shrubs with gold foliage denoted its eyes and a straggling group of red-leaved plants might have been its fiery breath. Its tail was missing and a path cut through one claw, yet it was still magnificent.

Enchanted, Luisa leaned a little further out.

She'd inherited her mother's love of gardens, though she'd had little time to indulge the interest.

Movement caught her eye. She looked up to see a familiar figure striding through the garden. Raul. Instantly, absurdly, her pulse fluttered.

He saw her and shouted something as he raced forward.

Instinctively Luisa recoiled, feeling as if she'd been caught trespassing. She pushed back and again that dizzy sensation hit. Only this time it wasn't just in her head.

To her horror, the wall beneath her hands shifted. Instead of rising up, her movement pushed her further out, the stone sliding forward with a terrible grinding noise.

She scrabbled back but her centre of gravity was too far forward. With a loud groan, the old sill tumbled out of her grasp to fall, with dreadful resounding thuds, to the ground below.

Luisa lurched forward, spreadeagled over jagged rock, her arms dangling into space and her eyes focused disbelievingly on the sheer drop below. Masonry bruised her ribs but she couldn't get breath to try inching back. Fear of another fall, this time with her in it, froze her.

She couldn't see Raul now and the staccato beat of blood in her ears drowned every sound. Her throat closed so she couldn't even yell for help. Swirling nausea made her head swim.

Her breath came in jerky gasps as she tried to crawl backwards, only to slide further forward as another block tumbled with a reverberating crash.

Any minute now, that could be her.

'It's all right.' The deep, soothing voice barely penetrated her consciousness. 'I've got you.' On the words strong arms slid beneath her waist.

'No!' she gasped, terror freezing her muscles. 'Keep back. It's too dangerous.' Surely Raul's weight with hers on the unstable wall would send them both plummeting.

'Don't move. Just relax and let me do this.'

'Relax?' He must be kidding. Luisa squeezed her eyes shut as swirling dots appeared in her vision.

Her body was rigid as he hauled her back, his arms locked around her. She waited, breathless, for the ominous groan of rock on rock. Instead she heard Raul's indrawn breath as he took her weight against him, dragging her slowly but inexorably to safety.

There was heat behind her. Searing heat that branded her back as he held her to him. His breath feathered her nape and his hands gripped so hard she wondered if she'd have bruises. But they'd be nothing to the bruises on her ribs from the stones. Or to her injuries if she'd fallen.

A shudder racked her and she squeezed her eyes even tighter, trying to block the pictures her mind conjured.

'Shh. It's all right. You're safe. I promise.' Yet the tremors wouldn't subside. Her teeth began to chatter.

Desperately she sought for composure. 'I n-never did l-like heights.'

'Open your eyes.' He held her away and the shaking worsened. Her eyes snapped open in protest but he was already lowering her to sit on the floor.

Luisa slumped like a rag doll, her bones water. Even now the view down to the distant flagstones was emblazoned on her brain.

'Here, lean forward.' She did as she was told and heat enveloped her as Raul draped his jacket around her quaking shoulders. A subtle spicy scent surrounded her. The scent of Raul's aftershave. Or perhaps the scent of him. Luisa breathed deep, letting the fragrance fill her lungs.

She lifted her head. He stood before her, hands on hips, brow pleated and mouth a stark line.

Luisa had seen him without a jacket only once, briefly, in the limo. Always he was impeccably dressed. It shocked her that beneath that tailored elegance was a broad chest of considerable power.

Her eyes trailed over his heaving torso, noting the way his stance drew the fine cotton of his shirt taut, moulding to a body that wasn't that of an effete clothes horse but a strong, very masculine man. Luisa's heart skittered to a new rhythm as she remembered that solid muscle pressed against her on the boat in Paris. No wonder he'd felt so good!

'We need to get you inside where it's warm.' Yet

he didn't move to help her rise. Did he see how weak she was?

Shakily she nodded, drawing his jacket close. 'Soon. I need to get my b-breath.' She had to pull herself together but she couldn't quite manage it.

'Here.' With a quick stride, Raul moved behind her. Next thing she knew, those capable hands were on her again. He pulled her up and across his lap as he sat leaning against the wall opposite the gap.

Luisa should protest. She didn't want to be this close to him. But she didn't have the energy to resist and had to be content holding herself as stiff as she could in his arms. As if she could ignore the heat of those solid, muscular thighs or his arms around her!

'I hope that wall's safe!'

'It's fine. Don't worry. It's only the other side that's a problem.' He hauled her closer so her shoulder was tucked into his chest. 'Didn't you see the warning sign?'

She recalled a neat sign at the base of the tower but she'd barely glanced at it.

'The door was unlocked.'

'It won't be in future.' His voice was grim. 'Not until it's safe.' He tugged her closer but she resisted. Any nearer and her head would be on his shoulder. The idea both attracted and horrified her.

'Why did you come up here? You get finer views from the other side of the castle.'

She shrugged jerkily. 'I wanted to see the parterre garden. Gregor showed it to me, but you don't get the effect from the ground.'

'Gregor?' A steely note in his voice made her turn and meet his eyes head-on. They had darkened to a shade of rich forest-green. This close she was surprised to find a glimmer of scintillating gold sprinkled there too.

'Yes.' She found she was leaning towards him and drew back abruptly. 'One of your gardeners. He showed me around.'

The frown returned to Raul's face and his mouth flattened. But, instead of marring his features, it made him look like a sulky angel.

A quiver began low in her stomach that had nothing to do with her recent scare.

'He didn't encourage you to come up here, did he?'

'Of course not.' It was only now she realised Gregor's gestures had been to warn her away from the unsafe structure.

'Thank you for saving me.' She should have thanked Raul immediately but her brain was too frazzled.

'I'm just glad I saw you when I did.' His hold

firmed and his frown became a scowl, as if he'd like to blame someone.

Luisa looked at his concerned expression and tried to remember how callous he was. That he'd forced her hand.

'Just think. If you hadn't reached me, you mightn't have had a princess to marry. Then you'd never inherit.'

A large firm hand cupped her jaw and cheek. His gaze snared hers and her breath caught. The gold in his eyes seemed to flare brighter. Or was that because he was nearer?

He shook his head slowly. 'If there was no princess, the contract would no longer bind me.' His thumb slid under her chin and Luisa's eyelashes fluttered as a strange lethargic heat stole through her. 'I'd have been free to marry whomever I want.'

'Is there someone you *want* to marry?' The notion clawed Luisa back from the brink of surrendering to his caress.

'Don't worry, Luisa.' His face loomed closer. 'You're not coming between me and the love of my life.'

'So there's no one special?' It confirmed his cold-blooded approach to marriage. But right now, dazzled by his brilliant stare, lulled by his rhythmic caress and the encompassing heat of his body,

Luisa couldn't scrape the energy to be outraged. She felt…distanced from pain. Who'd have thought she'd find solace in Raul's embrace? There was unexpected pleasure in the sense that, for this moment at least, they could be frank.

'No one who matters.' His warm breath caressed her face and she struggled to find the anger that had burned within her before. Surely she shouldn't enjoy being here, with him.

'You really are ruthless, aren't you?' Her tone was conversational, curious, rather than accusing.

It was as if, after the shock of her accident, she floated on another plane where all that mattered was that she was safe in Raul's strong arms.

He shifted and she found her head lolling against his shoulder, his body cradling hers. She almost sighed at how good that felt. She felt boneless, like a cat being stroked in the sun.

'If you mean that I plan to get what I want, then yes.' His lips curved in a smile that held something other than humour. His intense focus reminded her of the way he'd watched her in Paris. Heat filled her.

'Have you always managed to get your own way?' She should protest about how he held her but it felt so good and Luisa liked this new, unreal world where she and Raul weren't at daggers drawn. Where that fragile connection shimmered in the still air.

He shook his head. 'Far from it. I was anything but spoiled. My mother died in childbirth and my father was impatient with children.'

Her heart clenched. No wonder Raul was so self-sufficient. She stared up at his perfectly sculpted mouth, just made for reducing women to mindless adoration.

'But as an adult. With women, I bet you've always—'

'Luisa.' The hand at her jaw slid round to thread through her hair and hold the back of her head. His eyes gleamed with an inner fire. 'You're talking too much.'

She watched those lips descend in slow motion. As if he gave her a chance to pull free. Or to savour their impending kiss. Excitement raced through her.

By the time his mouth covered hers Luisa's breath had stalled, her lips opening to meet his, her pulse an insistent, urgent beat.

Their kiss was slow, a leisurely giving and receiving of pleasure. Delight swamped her in a warm, sultry wave. This wasn't like the forceful, hungry passion they'd shared in Paris.

A voice in her head tried to point out that in Paris they'd shared nothing. Raul hadn't felt anything.

But Paris seemed so far away.

Here, now, this felt like something shared. Something offered and accepted. Not dominance or submission. Not demand or acquiescence, but something utterly, satisfyingly mutual.

Luisa slipped an arm around his waist, revelling in how his muscles tensed then relaxed to her touch, testament to the leashed power of the man caressing her so gently. The realisation heightened her pleasure.

His tongue curled against hers as he drew her deeper into his mouth and the little voice of sanity subsided, overwhelmed by the magic Raul wove with his kiss, his big body, his tenderness.

Desire unfurled within her like a bud opening to the sunlight. Tendrils spread low to the feminine hollow between her legs. Up to her breasts that tingled as he pulled her closer, as if to absorb her into his body.

Her other hand rose to splay across his neck, discovering the pulse thudding heavily at his jaw. Then up to tangle in the rough silk of his hair.

Raul growled at the back of his throat. The raw sound of pleasure thrilled across her skin and sent heat plunging through her.

The languor that had held her spellbound dissipated and she wriggled against him, wanting more. The tingle of sensation at her hardening nipples became a prickle of need. The lavish, slow swirling eddy of delight in her belly grew more urgent.

Then, abruptly, he pulled back. Just enough for her to see his face. Stunned, it took a moment to read the heat in his hooded gaze and realise he was breathing heavily.

He grasped her wrist and tugged it down, holding it securely away from him.

'Next time—' his nostrils flared as he drew a deep breath '—if you want a tour, ask me. I'll arrange to come with you or have someone guide you. Agreed?'

Silently Luisa nodded, her mind abuzz, her world rocked out of kilter. Could she blame shock for the fact that she wanted to fall back into the arms of the man she'd been so sure she detested?

Two weeks later, in conversation with a gallery curator, Raul found his gaze straying to Luisa. She stood before a display of botanical studies, talking to the junior curator who'd organised the exhibit.

Raul's gaze slid appreciatively up her slender legs. It was the first time he'd seen her in a dress and he couldn't keep his eyes off her. Especially when she smiled at her companion with all the warmth of her sunny homeland.

The impact was stunning. Heat flickered along his veins and pooled in his groin.

She was blossoming into a lovely woman. That had to explain why she'd been knotting his belly with thwarted desire since Paris.

And why he'd succumbed to temptation and kissed her in the tower. His pulse jumped and a spike of something like fear drove through his chest at the memory of her sprawled out over that fatal drop. The need to hold her and not release her had been unstoppable. The hunger for another sweet taste of her lips inexplicable.

It disturbed him, the force of this unexpected attraction.

She was utterly unlike his usual companions. She was unpolished, preferring flats to high heels and avoiding even the simplest of her inherited jewellery. She had a habit of talking to anyone, particularly the staff, rather than to VIPs. He sensed she'd be as happy chatting to the gardeners as attending a glitzy premiere occasion.

Yet his heart lifted when he was with her.

He told himself that was sentimental twaddle. Yet there was definitely *something* about his bride-to-be.

Raul shook his head. Didn't he prefer his women sophisticated, assured and sexy?

Why did Luisa infiltrate his thoughts at every turn? Why had he found it so hard to release her that day in the tower? Or to pursue his own busy agenda while she began her lessons in language, etiquette, history and culture?

Because he wanted her. And, almost as much as he wanted her, he wanted her company.

Raul turned to his companion. 'Could the Princess and I have time alone to view the rest of the exhibition?'

The curator agreed enthusiastically. Such interest boded well. Two minutes later Raul and Luisa were alone. Even the guard at the door discreetly melted into an adjoining space.

'Thank you.' She turned to him and he saw her eyes were overbright. His heart thumped an unfamiliar beat and his hand closed automatically over hers.

'Are you OK?' He'd thought to please her with this visit, not upset her. Show her she *did* have a connection with his homeland.

'I didn't expect to see my mum's work on show. It was a lovely surprise.'

Raul shrugged. 'She was a talented artist. It's a shame she didn't continue her botanical painting.'

Luisa looked away. 'She dabbled but she said it was a discipline that needed dedication. She couldn't give that. Not with the farm.'

He nodded. It was clear what a toll that place had taken on Luisa's family. Her mother should have more than early works on display. She would have if she'd not embraced a life of hardship. All for the supposed love of a man who could give her so little.

People were fools, falling for the fantasy of love.

So-called love was an illusion. A trap for the unwary. Hadn't he learnt that to his cost?

'It was kind of you to bring me.' She touched his sleeve and looked up from under her lashes in an unconsciously provocative way that made heat curl in his gut. 'Lukas told me you rarely have time for such things, especially now.'

'It was nothing. It's been a while since I visited and there were issues to discuss.' The last thing he needed was for her to get the idea he'd changed his schedule for her. Even if it was true.

Luisa had been stoically uncomplaining through her first weeks in Maritz. Yet the change must be difficult for her. Despite her heavy tuition sched-ule he'd often glanced up from a meeting to see her wandering in the gardens and he had the discomfiting notion she was lonely, despite her ever-widening acquaintance.

Guilt blanketed him. She was here because of him, his country, his needs. What did she personally get out of it?

She wasn't interested in riches or prestige. The only money she wanted was to save her friends.

His lips twisted. She didn't see *him* as a prize, even if she couldn't conceal the passion that flared when he kissed her. Luisa Hardwicke was a salutary lesson to his ego.

'I had no idea Mum's work was so well regarded.' She turned to examine a delicate drawing of a mountain wildflower and he followed, not wanting to lose the warmth of her hand on his arm.

'Tell me about her.'

Luisa swung round. 'Why?'

He shrugged, making light of his sudden need to understand Luisa's family, and her. 'She must have been strong to have stood up to your grandfather.'

Luisa grimaced. 'Maybe it's a family trait.'

'Sorry?'

She shook her head. 'I thought she was remarkable. And so did my dad.'

Raul threaded his fingers through hers, pleased when she didn't pull away. 'Tell me.'

For a long moment she regarded him. Then she seemed to make up her mind. 'She was like other mums. Hard working, making do, running a household and doing the books. Always busy.' Luisa paused. 'She made the best cinnamon Christmas biscuits and she gave the warmest hugs—guaranteed to make you feel better every time. She loved roses and had an eye for fashion, even if we couldn't afford to buy it.'

Luisa moved to the next picture and he followed. 'She hated ironing and she *detested* getting up early.'

'Not suited to be a farmer's wife then.' The change from palace to dairy must have been hard. Had the marriage been a disaster? He frowned. It didn't sound so.

Luisa laughed, a rich, lilting chuckle and Raul's senses stirred. 'That's what Dad used to say. He'd shake his head and pretend to be scared she'd go back to her glamorous world. Mum would smile that special smile she saved for him and say she couldn't possibly leave till she mastered the art of cooking sponge cakes as well as my aunt. Dad would say no one could ever make sponges like Mary, so Mum would just have to stay for ever. Then he'd kiss her.'

Raul felt the delicate tremor in her hand and

watched a wistful smile flit across Luisa's features. He knew an unaccountable desire to experience what she had. The warmth, the love. A childhood of cinnamon biscuits and hugs. How different from his own upbringing!

'But how did it work?' He found himself curious. 'They were so different.'

She shrugged. 'They came from different worlds but they made their own together. Dad said she made him feel like a king. Mum always said he made her feel more like a princess than she'd ever felt living in a palace.' Luisa swung to face him. 'Life with my grandfather wasn't pleasant. He tried to force her into marrying someone she detested, just to cement a deal. There was no laughter, no fun. Not like in our home.'

Someone she detested. Did Raul fit that category for Luisa? He told himself the country must come first, yet he couldn't squash regret.

'They were in love; that was the secret.'

It didn't take a genius to know that was what Luisa had wanted for herself. Till he'd come along.

Never before had Raul's duty seemed so onerous. He was doomed to disappoint her. He didn't even believe in love. He'd never experienced it.

'But she loved it here.' Luisa turned to him, her

smile a shade too bright. 'Mum wanted to bring us one day to see it.'

'I'm glad.' He paused, clasping her hand more firmly. 'In time I hope you come to love it too. It's a special place. There are no people like Maritzians.'

'You're not biased, are you?'

'Surely that's my prerogative.' He led her towards the rest of the exhibition, regaling her with a traditional local story. It surprised him how much he wanted to hear her laugh again.

Raul strode swiftly to his study. There was a crushing amount of work to do and, though the unrest in the provinces had abated a little, he couldn't afford to be complacent.

Yet the wedding tomorrow, a small affair since the nation was in mourning for his father, would pave the way for his coronation and go a long way to solving his problems.

Taking his bride to bed would go a long way towards easing the permanent ache in his groin.

Anticipation pulsed in his blood at the thought of his wedding night to come. His desire for Luisa grew daily.

The more time he spent with his bride-to-be the more she fascinated him. She was vibrant, engaging, determinedly independent and down-to-earth. Different from every other woman he knew.

Even now he never knew what to expect from her.

Lukas approached as he reached the study.

'Your Highness.' He fell into step beside Raul.

'Yes? Am I late for my meeting?'

'No, not that.' His secretary hesitated, his mouth turning down. 'You have a visitor. I wanted to warn—'

'Raul. Darling!' The husky female voice came from the door ahead. For one shattered instant Raul felt his feet rivet to the floor as shock vibrated through him. His hands clenched into fists. Then, bracing himself, he slowly approached the blonde draped in the doorway.

'This is unexpected, Ana. What are you doing here?'

'Surely you didn't expect me to miss your wedding, darling?' She straightened and lifted her head, her lips a crimson pout. 'Your invitation didn't reach me. Luckily I heard about it on the grapevine.'

He stopped a metre away, distaste prickling his skin. Foolishly, he'd thought he'd seen the last of her, for the time being at least.

They weren't in public so there was no need for

a courteous bow. And she could wait till hell froze over before he took up the invitation implicit in that pout.

Not when she was the woman who eight years ago had dragged him to hell.

CHAPTER SEVEN

'LUISA, you look so lovely!' Tamsin said. 'This pearly cream is wonderful with the golden tone of your skin.'

'You think so?' Luisa stood stiffly, uncomfortable in the full length gown of silk. The fitted bodice covered with cobweb-fine hand-made lace. The diadem of finely wrought gold and pearls.

The bridal dress showcased the finest traditional Maritzian products. Lace from one province. Hand woven silk from another. The exquisite filigree gold choker necklace that made her throat seem elegant and impossibly fragile was by craftsmen in yet another province. Beaded slippers from still another.

Only the bride hadn't been involved in the design of her wedding clothes.

Gingerly Luisa turned to the mirror, feeling a fraud under the weight of this charade.

Yet the image awaiting her took her breath away. Could that really be *her*? A woman who till recently had spent her days in jeans and gumboots?

'You look like a fairy princess.' Tamsin shook a fold of embossed silk so the flaring skirt draped perfectly.

'I don't feel like it.' Nausea churned in Luisa's stomach. It was only through sheer willpower that she'd nibbled at a fruit platter for lunch. She whose appetite was always healthy!

'Believe me.' Tamsin clasped her hand briefly and smiled. 'You'll take everyone's breath away. Especially Raul. He won't be able to take his eyes off you.'

Luisa saw the other woman's secret smile and wondered if she was thinking of her recent marriage to Prince Alaric, Raul's distant cousin. It was clear that the big man with the steely jaw and face almost as handsome as Raul's was deeply in love with his new English wife.

For a moment Luisa let herself imagine what it would be like to marry for love. Burnt so badly years ago, she'd buried herself on the farm, shunning any hint of male interest. She'd longed to experience true love but had she been too craven to open herself to the possibility?

The day Raul had saved her from falling and kissed her so tenderly she'd allowed herself to be swept along by his deep voice, his gentle hands and the unstoppable cravings that welled at his touch.

For one fragile interlude she'd longed to believe something warm and special could grow from their union.

Then there was his unexpected kindness, taking her to see her mother's work.

But the fantasy was too painful. It scraped too close to the bone for a woman who'd been chosen, not for love or respect. Not even for convenience. But because Raul had no other option!

'It's good of you to help me get ready.' She sent a shaky smile in Tamsin's direction. Though this wasn't a romantic match it was her wedding day. The day women looked to their mother for support.

Luisa had never missed her mum more.

'It will be all right.' Again Tamsin took her hand, chafing warmth into it. 'I know how daunting it is marrying into a new world. Marrying royalty. But Raul will look after you. He's like my Alaric. Strong and protective.' She sent a speculative glance at Luisa. 'And I suspect behind that well bred calm, very passionate.'

Heat roared through Luisa's cheeks, banishing the chill that had frozen her all day.

Tamsin giggled, blushing herself. 'Sorry. I didn't mean to embarrass you. It's just sometimes I feel like pinching myself. It all seems so unreal!'

'I know what you mean.' Tamsin was an outsider

too—a commoner and a foreigner who'd married her prince in a love match that had intrigued everyone. But Tamsin had fallen in love. Luisa would face her royal marriage and the weight of public expectation without love to cushion the shock. Their circumstances were so different.

'I'm glad you're here,' she added, grateful to this initially reserved but warm-hearted woman.

'So am I! And when you settle in, after your honeymoon, I hope we can spend more time together.'

Luisa nodded, not bothering to disabuse her. Raul was a workaholic. That was why the trip to the gallery had been such a lovely surprise. He wouldn't take time off for a honeymoon. Not with a wife he didn't really want.

A wife who was simply a solution to a problem.

A cold lump of lead settled in the pit of her belly as a soft knock sounded on the door.

'It's time, Your Highness.'

The music swelled and the massive doors swung open and Luisa stepped over the threshold into the castle chapel.

Multicoloured streams of light shone through ancient windows. A cloying wave of fragrance hit. Hothouse flowers and incense and a multitude of perfumes. Hundreds of faces turned to stare. She didn't know a single one.

A rising tide of panic clawed at her, urging her to turn tail and run, as fast and as far as she could. Her heart slammed against her ribs and her knees shook.

She faltered, her hand curling into Alaric's sleeve. He covered her hand with his and leaned close. 'Luisa?'

'This is a *small* wedding?' Dazed, she saw heraldic banners, including some of the Maritzian red dragon, streaming from the lofty ceiling. The crowd murmured and it sounded like a roar.

'Courage, little one. It'll soon be over.' He paced forward and she had no option but to follow. 'Tamsin and I have a bet on who spots the most absurd hat. Weddings incite women to wear the most monstrous things on their heads, don't you think?'

His *sotto voce* patter continued all the way down the aisle, almost distracting her from the throng of hungry-eyed guests. Watching. Judging. Finding her wanting.

Suddenly she caught a smile. Tamsin, in muted gold, giving her an encouraging nod. Behind her was another woman, platinum blonde, dripping jewels yet sour-mouthed.

Then, abruptly, they were at the end of the aisle. Bands of steel squeezed the breath from her lungs as, with a sense of inescapable inevitability, she turned her head towards the dark figure she'd avoided since she entered.

Raul, tall and heart-stoppingly handsome in a uniform of scarlet and black that made him look like the model for Prince Charming.

Something in her chest rose and swelled. Was it possible that perhaps they could make this work? The other day they'd surely started building a fragile relationship.

Then she read his expression. Austere, proud, stern. Not a scintilla of pleasure. A complete absence of anything that might one day turn into love. His mouth was a stern line, his jaw chiselled rock.

She blinked quickly, hating herself because even now, faced with his indifference, she yearned for the tenderness he'd begun to show her.

How could she? She knew what she was to him. How could she be so weak as to want the impossible?

Luisa gulped. It was like swallowing shards of glass.

Just as well she hadn't allowed herself to pretend he reciprocated her inconvenient attraction.

Her hand tightened, talon-like as Alaric ushered

her forward. But Raul took her hand in his, his other hand at her elbow as she swayed.

She had to quell this anxiety. She'd *agreed* to this. She looked away, to the mass of flowers by the altar: a riot of roses, orange blossom and lilies. Their scent was too pungent for her roiling stomach.

The priest spoke but Luisa didn't listen. She was thinking that at home lilies were traditional for funerals.

'Who *is* that woman?' Luisa watched the petite platinum blonde lean into Raul, her hand possessive on his arm. Her scarlet dress matched his jacket perfectly and her plunging neckline showed a stunning cleavage. She smiled up, her face hardly recognisable as the one that had scowled at Luisa in the chapel.

'She wasn't in the reception line,' Luisa added.

Raul stood on the other side of the reception room, his back to Luisa, but from here she'd almost swear the woman flirted with him. A spike of heat roared through her. Heat and anger. 'Is she an ex-girlfriend?'

Beside her Tamsin spluttered, choking on champagne.

'Are you OK?'

Tamsin waved her away. 'I inhaled some bubbles. I'm not used to champagne.'

Luisa knew the feeling. This evening she'd sipped some, standing beside Raul for a formal toast. The wine had tickled her senses and tingled all the way down her throat. But it was Raul's presence beside her, like a wall of living heat, that had made her giddy. His stern expression had eased for a moment and his lips had curved in a heady smile as he toasted her. The impact had knocked her for six and Luisa had felt as if she were floating.

As if this were a real wedding and she a bride smitten with her handsome husband! Instead of a woman blackmailed into cooperating. That still rankled.

Luisa stiffened. It scared her that Raul affected her so. That she might be jealous of the woman pawing at his jacket. It should be impossible, yet…

'You don't know her?'

Finally Tamsin looked up. A flush tinted her cheeks.

'Tamsin?' Her new friend's expression made Luisa tense.

'The woman with Raul? No one you need worry about.' The words came out in a rush. 'She lives in the US now.'

'But who *is* she?'

Tamsin took another quick sip of wine. 'That's Ana. Raul's stepmother.'

Stepmother?

'But she's too young!' She didn't act like a step-mother. The other woman was flirting outra-geously. Luisa's only consolation came from the fact Raul stood as stiffly as he had through the wedding ceremony, though he inclined his head as if listening intently.

'I think she and Raul are about the same age.'

Through her shock Luisa heard Tamsin's intense discomfort. She saw Tamsin's gaze dart away as if seeking a diversion and uneasiness stirred.

Intuition told her there was something Tamsin wasn't saying. Luisa turned back, finally noticing how the guests kept their distance from the pair. No one had approached Raul since his stepmother had claimed his attention but they all watched specula-tively. An undercurrent of whispers eddied around them.

The frisson of uneasiness grew to stark suspicion.

No! Luisa refused to draw conclusions about Raul's relationships. No matter what her eyes told her.

Yet she couldn't stifle a feeling of betrayal.

As if sensing her scrutiny, Raul turned sharply,

his gaze skewering her. Fire seared her blood and she felt as if she'd been caught out spying on him.

But she had every right to be here. This was *her* wedding reception. *Her* day. Even if it wasn't her choice.

Hysterical laughter bubbled in her throat. Today should be the happiest day of her life!

If she didn't laugh at the absurdity surely she'd cry.

Holding Raul's eyes, she lifted her chin and downed the rest of her champagne.

'If you'll excuse me, Tamsin, I'd better introduce myself to my mother-in-law.' Luisa passed her glass to a waiter and picked up her skirts, grateful now for the formal dress that kept her posture perfect and made guests move aside as she stalked forward.

She was magnificent. She cut a swathe through the crowd as if it didn't exist, her eyes locked with his.

A pulse of heat thudded deep in his belly at the sight of her: jaw angled, eyes glittering, chest swelling against the demure V neckline. She skimmed across the polished floor, her train sweeping magnificently behind her. Tiny bursts of fire peeped from beneath her hem as her jewel-encrusted slippers caught the light. It was as if she set off sparks with each step.

Absently Raul brushed Ana's clawing hand away. He'd done what he had to—accepted her presence publicly. But he'd had enough.

He'd had enough of her eight years ago!

He barely registered her protest as he strode instead towards the woman he'd just married and pleasure surged.

All day tension had ridden him. Worries for the state. Fury at Ana's return. Discomfort at the idea of marrying. Guilt at forcing Luisa's hand. The need to bury his thoughts deep behind a cloak of royal calm. Now the tension morphed into something that had nothing to do with concerns and everything to do with his long-suppressed needs.

And with the challenge he read in his bride's expression, her posture, her firmed lips.

Her eyes flashed azure fire and heat danced in his veins. He drew a breath, the first free breath all day.

He'd done his duty in marrying. Now he wanted to forget about duty, about diplomacy and building bridges with intransigent politicians and soothing the bruised egos of his father's cronies. About his own doubts.

He wanted...Luisa.

A smile cracked his carefully schooled features.

'Luisa, you look enchanting.' Her pace propelled her forward and he took full advantage, stepping before her at the last moment and putting a hand to her waist, ostensibly to steady her. Through the lace and silk he felt warmth and lithe muscle and the deep exhalation of her breath.

He grasped her other hand in his and lifted it to his mouth. Her eyes blazed and he almost smiled at the provocation in her glare. Instead he turned her hand and pressed his lips to her wrist. He heard her breath catch and a satisfying tremor rippled through her. Slowly he moved his mouth, kissing her palm and touching his tongue to the erogenous zone at its centre.

Her eyes widened and he felt pleasure tug through his belly. She tried to draw her hand away but he held her.

'Aren't you going to introduce me to your mother?'

He read the doubt and hurt pride in her eyes and silently applauded her front.

'You mean my father's second wife. Not my mother.'

'My mistake.' She bit the words out precisely with her even white teeth. 'You two looked so close...'

Little cat.

This was what he'd missed. Much as he enjoyed having his plans go smoothly and the tantalising sense of closeness he'd experienced with Luisa now and then, he'd missed her vibrancy. From the first she'd sparked with energy and defiance. She'd obstructed him and argued and defied him. Even consenting to wed she'd been proud as an empress.

He enjoyed her sassiness when she stood up to him. He'd grown accustomed to fireworks. He enjoyed them more than he'd thought possible. Especially when it wasn't argument that fuelled the conflagration.

Even the hint of jealousy in her tone pleased him. Did her desire match his? A bolt of excitement shot through him. He recalled her passion, the way she melted in his arms. How she watched him when she thought he didn't see.

He leaned forward and whispered, 'I'm not going to introduce her. You wouldn't like her.'

She gaped at his honesty. He wanted to kiss those lush lips till she forgot how to speak. He wanted that sizzling energy channelled in more satisfying directions.

Urgent heat swirled in his loins as he visualised it.

'Why not?' Luisa looked stunned.

'Because she's not at all nice.' It surprised him

how much pleasure there was in saying it out loud, even if in a murmur for Luisa's ears alone. How long he'd been constrained by the need to keep up appearances!

'But surely I need to meet her.'

'Hardly. She's leaving for LA tonight. Grabbing a lift with her newest boyfriend, a Hollywood producer.'

Raul didn't even feel the usual simmering anger. Ana couldn't be bothered to feign mourning for her dead husband. Their marriage had been a farce, his smitten father turning a blind eye to anything in his young wife's behaviour that might dent his royal pride.

Raul was tired of pretending his father's marriage was anything but a sham. His father was dead and his ego couldn't be battered any more. Ana didn't deserve more than the merest observance of courtesy. Her attempt just now to wheedle more cash from the royal coffers had been expected but her timing had surprised even Raul, who'd believed himself inured to her grasping ways.

'Come,' he said, turning Luisa with him towards the dais where the royal throne rested. She grabbed her wide skirts and followed. The scent of lavender that accompanied her movements was refreshing after Ana's cloying perfume. He breathed deep and helped his wife up the steps.

The flush colouring Luisa's cheeks was charming. His gaze descended her throat, gorgeous in its gold filigree and pearl choker, down to where her breasts rose and fell rapidly. His palms itched to touch.

Leaving the reception early would cause a stir. But he wasn't in the mood to worry about protocol. After years acceding to duty and convention, trying to compensate for the trauma of earlier royal scandal, Raul chose for the first time to flout tradition.

It felt good. The gossips could go hang.

He reached for his wife's hand, enjoying the way it fitted his own so neatly. Enjoying her presence beside him.

'Highnesses, ladies and gentlemen.' Raul addressed the assembly. When he'd finished the sound of clapping made him turn. There were Alaric and Tamsin, smiling broadly. The applause spread.

Raul raised a hand in acknowledgement, then turned to Luisa. 'It's time we left.'

Her eyes rounded but a moment later she conjured a smile and a wave for their audience. She really was superb.

A moment later Raul ushered her out through

the double doors behind the throne, held open by footmen.

Then they were walking down the private corridor, her hand still in his. The doors closed behind them, muting the swell of applause.

Satisfaction filled him. He was alone with his bride.

It happened so quickly Luisa was dazed as he led her through the labyrinth of corridors.

Only two things were real. Raul's warm hand enfolding hers and the fact she was married. Even in the chapel it hadn't seemed real. But hearing Raul tell their guests to enjoy their wedding hospitality, seeing the curiosity, the goodwill, even the envy on some of the faces staring up at her, it had suddenly hit.

She'd bound herself to this man. No turning back.

Her spurt of indignation over his stepmother dwindled. Now she felt only shock.

Raul's hand tightened and sensation streaked through her.

No, she felt more than shock. A tiny bud of something curled tight inside. Something that kept her hand in his even when she knew she should withdraw it. Something that shortened her breath as

Raul halted before an unfamiliar door then stood aside, waiting for her to precede him.

She stepped in then halted. She shouldn't be here in his private apartments.

The door closed, silence enveloping them. Her breathing was overloud as she sought for something to say.

'Come.' A hand at her elbow propelled her forward. 'You need food. You ate nothing at the reception.'

'How do you know?' For much of the reception they'd been on opposite sides of the room.

'I watched you.'

She started, stunned at the idea of Raul concentrating on her all the time he'd chatted with dignitaries. The notion sent a ribbon of heat through her.

'And you had just one glass of champagne.'

Her gaze melded with his. The kindling heat she saw made her look hastily away.

'Maybe a bite of something would be a good idea.' Then she'd go. She felt too aware of him beside her.

Aware of herself too, in a new, unsettling way. Of the swish of rich fabric around her legs as she moved. Of the tight clasp of the fitted bodice at her waist and breasts as she struggled to draw in oxygen. The fabric of her bra seemed suddenly abrasive, drawing her nipples to taut peaks.

She stepped away, only to stop again abruptly. Her eyes widened. 'This looks…intimate.' It sounded like an accusation.

'Does it matter?'

'Of course it matters!' Luisa bit her lip at her high pitched response. She sounded like a schoolgirl, not a mature woman.

A low table was drawn up before a massive sofa long enough for even Raul to recline full length. Velvet cushions made it look plush and inviting. A foil-topped bottle nestled in a silver cooler. Cold lobster lay sumptuously arrayed beside a bowl of fresh ice that cradled gleaming beads of caviar.

Luisa stepped back abruptly, only to find Raul behind her. She spun round, hands planted on his chest as if to ward him off. So why did her fingers curl into his jacket?

Hurriedly she retreated. 'Is this someone's idea of a joke? It's like a clichéd set for a seduction.'

'You don't like lobster?'

'Well, yes.' She'd only tried it here in the castle and had loved every mouthful.

'Or fruit?' He gestured and she spied a platter of her favourite fruits: peaches and cherries and glowing navel oranges. Beside them was a bowl of fresh berries. Beyond that a basket of bread rolls—not the fine dinner rolls that graced the royal table but the malty whole-grain bread, thick with seeds, that she'd discovered when she'd invited herself to the kitchens. Traditional peasant fare, she was told. The best bread she'd tasted.

Luisa leaned closer. Beyond that were fat curls of butter, a board of cheeses and a silver bowl of cashews. Her favourites.

A familiar jar at the end of the table caught her eye. Mary's spidery writing on the label: raspberry jam.

Luisa blinked hard, her pulse thudding. She reached out and stroked the thick glass jar of her aunt's home-made jam, the jam she'd been helping make since she was a child. A taste of home. Luisa could barely believe he'd taken the trouble to ask Mary for this.

Raul hadn't just clapped his hands and ordered a feast. This was just for her. Something special. His unexpected thoughtfulness blindsided her.

'How did you...?' Her throat closed on emotion.

'How did I know you prefer fruit to gateaux, cheeses to chocolate?'

Shaken, Luisa turned. He stood so close she saw again that sparkle of gold in his dark green gaze.

'Because I notice everything about you.' His

voice was deliciously deep. 'You are my wife now. I want you to be happy.' The warmth in his tone made her tremble inside.

Not even to herself would she admit how those words eased her wounded soul.

'But not like *this*.' Her wide gesture encompassed the sofa, the crystal flutes, the whole seductive scene. 'We agreed to a marriage of convenience!'

Was she trying to convince herself or him? From the moment she'd stepped into his chamber she'd had the delicious sense of walking on a knife-edge of excitement.

Raul said nothing. Yet his look heated her skin. His mouth was a sensual line of temptation she had to resist.

Luisa's heart drummed an urgent tattoo. Part of her wanted nothing more than to touch him. To feel his power beneath her hand. That was why she forced her hands behind her back and kept them there.

Did he read her desire? His brilliant green eyes were hot with an inner blaze and Luisa realised how close she came to being singed.

'We married for legal reasons.' Her words were slurred because her tongue was glued to the roof of her mouth. 'So you can inherit. Remember?'

'I remember.' His voice was low, resonating

through her body to places she didn't know existed before. 'I remember how it felt to kiss you too. Do you recall that, Luisa? The fire between us? The need?'

She shook her head and her veil swirled between them. It snagged on the gold braiding that marched across his tunic, emphasising the breadth of his chest.

'It wasn't like that. You just…'

Her throat closed as he untangled her veil. His fingers were centimetres from her breast and she sucked her breath in, trying not to think of him touching her there.

But breathing meant movement. Her breast brushed his hand. She gasped as sensation pierced her and she trembled.

He didn't look up but she saw his lips curve.

'I'm not some passing amusement.' She gritted her teeth, trying not to breathe too heavily.

'I never thought you were. I take you much too seriously for that.' His eyes snared hers and she forgot about breathing. His hands dropped away to hold hers, warm and firm. 'You are my bride. You'll be the mother of my children. I don't take you lightly at all.'

His mouth curved up in the sort of smile mothers had warned their daughters about for centuries.

Luisa felt its impact like a judder of power right down to the soles of her feet.

Her heart raced—in indignation she assured herself. Yet indignation had nothing to do with the hunger coiling inside or the febrile heat flooding her body.

'I never agreed to share your bed.'

She tried to summon anger but discovered instead a jittery thrill of dangerous excitement.

'You don't want children?' His brows rose.

'Of course I want—' She stopped and tried to harness her skittering thoughts. 'One day.' Once she'd dreamed of a family. But with Raul? She'd thought this a paper marriage. Or had she deliberately deceived herself? Heat poured across her skin and eddied deep in her womb.

The trouble was he tempted her with the very thing she'd tried unsuccessfully to deny wanting: him. From the first she'd been unable to prevent herself responding to him at the most basic level.

He took desire for granted but for her it was momentous. Life-changing. She'd learnt distrust too young.

His smile would reduce a lesser woman to a puddle of longing. Luisa it merely turned to jelly. Her knees gave way with a suddenness that astounded her.

Why didn't it surprise her when he swept her up against his chest in one fluid, easy move?

'I never said…'

He crossed the room as if she weighed nothing, entering another chamber and kicking shut the door. This room held a wide bed that seemed to stretch for hectares. The sight of it dried her mouth.

He lowered her and Luisa shut her eyes, wishing she didn't delight in the friction of each slow, tormenting centimetre as she slid against him.

'I thought you had spirit, Luisa. Why are you afraid?' His tone sharpened. 'Did someone hurt you?'

Her eyes snapped open at his husky anger.

'No. I wasn't hurt.' Not physically at least.

Yet he was right. She was afraid: of these new overwhelming feelings. Afraid she'd lose herself if she gave in to this longing. That it was a betrayal of her moral code—giving herself to a man she didn't love.

Yet standing here, bereft now of his touch, feeling the heat of his breath on her face and his body so close, desire twisted deep. Hunger for an intimacy she'd never had. Would never have with love, not now she'd given herself in a cold, practical bargain.

He'd robbed her of that chance.

The realisation was an icy hand on her heart.

She'd never experience true love. Would never have what her parents had shared. That was what she'd always hoped for, especially after the disaster of her first romance.

The knowledge doused her fears and made her angry as never before. Scorching fury rose, stronger than regret or doubt.

Raul had taken so much from her.

'Is it so wrong to find pleasure together?' He voiced the thoughts that already ran, pure temptation, through her head. 'You disappoint me, Luisa. I thought you woman enough to admit what you feel.'

Luisa stared up into his hot gaze and wanted nothing more than to wipe away his smug self-satisfaction. For him desire was easy. No longing for love. No doubts or fears.

A tumble of images cascaded in her head. Turning on her heel and storming out. Or walking serenely, with a cool pitying expression on her face as she left him behind. None of them did justice to the roiling tide of emotion he'd unleashed.

Instead Luisa stepped in, slamming hard against his body. She took his face in her palms and kissed him full on the mouth. She leaned in to him till, with a flurry of billowing silk, they collapsed onto the bed.

CHAPTER EIGHT

IT WAS like holding a flame, or a bolt of lightning.

Luisa was all urgent energy. Her touch, her body, igniting explosions in his blood.

Sensation speared through him. White light flickered behind his eyelids as she pushed her tongue into his mouth in an angry, urgent mating. There was little finesse but her hunger incited the most possessive urges.

She grabbed his scalp as if to imprison him with her scorching passion.

Raul welcomed it, meeting her questing tongue in a desperate kiss that was more like a battle for supremacy than a caress.

He felt alive as never before, caught by a throbbing force that drove every thought from his head but one.

The need for Luisa. Now.

He growled in his throat as he lashed one arm around her waist and the other lower, clamping his hand on her bunched skirts to pull her tight against his groin as he sank back on the wide bed. He was on fire.

Splayed over him, she wriggled as if she too couldn't get close enough. He pushed his hips up and felt her legs slide satisfyingly wide to surround him.

Yes!

It was as if she'd smashed the lock on his self-control. All those primitive urges that he, as a civilised man, had learned to suppress, roared to the surface, stripped bare by this woman who kissed as if she hated him.

He knew passion, used it as a release from the difficulties of life under the spotlight. But never had it been this blistering current of untrammelled power.

Again he rocked up into her encompassing heat and she pushed down to meet him with a jerky movement that spoke of need rather than grace.

Raul scrabbled at the mass of her skirts, pulling it higher and higher around her back till finally he touched silky bare skin. His pulse throbbed in his throat and his groin simultaneously as he clamped both hands to the taut warm silk over her backside. He could almost swear flames crackled around them.

The sound of her cry, a wordless mew of encouragement against his mouth, notched the tension impossibly higher.

Holding her tight, he drew her pelvis to his in a circling movement and sparks ignited in his blood.

A moment later he had her on her back, a tumble of silk and lace and femininity. Hands around her slim waist, he tugged her higher up the bed with a strength born of urgency.

She was flushed, her eyes a narrow glitter of heaven, her lips open and inviting as she gulped in air. Her breasts strained against the tight bodice and he allowed himself a moment's diversion. He covered one breast with his hand, feeling her arch into his touch, her nipple a pebbled tease to his palm. He rotated his hand, squeezing gently and she groaned, her eyes slitting shut and her body moving restlessly.

With his other hand Raul was already busy scooping metres of silk up and away to uncover her calves, her thighs. But a man could do two things at once. He ducked his head and kissed her open-mouthed on the breast, drawing lace and silk and her hard little nipple against his tongue.

Her hands clamped his head close and her breath was a hiss of delight. Beneath him she twisted and bucked as if seeking the weight of his body on hers.

He'd never had a woman so wild for him. No

games, no subtlety, just a devastating need that matched his own.

Such pure passion was liberating.

Raul let his hand skim up Luisa's thighs to her panties, pressing hard and discovering damp proof of her need. It was all the encouragement he required.

Seconds later he'd loosened his trousers and freed himself enough to slide his length against her hot apex in a move so arousing he had to pause and gather his scattered wits.

Luisa wouldn't wait. She circled her hips in hungry little movements that tore at the last vestige of his control.

Propped on one arm, Raul ripped away the delicate fabric of her panties and settled himself on her.

'Is this what you want?' His voice was thick, rough with desire and the promise of unsurpassed pleasure.

Azure fire blazed from her eyes. He read passion and something fierce and unfamiliar. But her body eased beneath him. She was enticingly soft, reassuringly strong and vibrating with erotic energy.

She panted for him yet he wanted to hear the words. Why, he had no idea.

He fitted one hand to her upthrust breast and felt her jolt beneath him.

'Tell me, Luisa.' He pushed against her, torturing himself as much as her with the luscious friction of body on body. 'What do you want?'

Her eyes widened and he felt himself sink into their brilliance. She rose, tugging his head down and her mouth took his, greedily, tongue swirling and plunging.

Raul struggled against the force of her ardour and his own pleasure. But it was too much. Too close.

With a muffled groan he gave in and reciprocated, tasting her, almost taming her mouth with his then retreating so the kiss became a mutual give and take of sensual combat.

Using his thighs, he nudged her legs wider and settled himself at her entrance. He slid one hand over blonde downy hair to find the nub of her pleasure. One stroke and she shivered. A second stroke and she shuddered.

'Raul!' His name was a tiny, breathless gasp that shattered his fragile control.

A moment later, his mouth claiming hers, he drove inside. Pressure screamed through him as tight, hot, silken walls enclosed him. Tighter than was surely possible. Raul felt her tremble around him, her raised thighs quaking against his hips.

Stunned, he made to draw back but Luisa fastened her hands in his hair and kissed him with a desperation that made his head swim. Or was that from the relief of finally being sheathed in her body?

She wrapped her legs around him and he sank deeper, lodging fully in exquisite pleasure. He braced himself as the trembling spread from her body to his, making his nape prickle and every muscle quake with tension.

It was no good. Stillness was impossible. Clamping his hands on her hips, he slid back, seeing stars behind closed eyelids as sensation rushed through him.

Another second and he thrust again, harder, longer, as he gave in to the force of a desire that had ridden him ever since that night in Paris.

'I'm sorry. I can't...' His words were swallowed by the roar of blood pounding in his ears.

Dimly he heard a cry rend the air. Luisa convulsed around him, tearing at his strength and his consciousness as he lost himself in delight.

Frantically his body pumped, driven by a force so strong only Luisa's gasps anchored him to reality.

His movements crescendoed, wringing out every last vestige of white-hot pleasure, till, with lungs bursting and the world spinning away, Raul sank into oblivion.

Despite his weight on her, Luisa felt as if she were floating. Echoes of incredible pleasure shimmered through limbs taut with the aftershock of tension.

Finally she gathered the strength to move a fraction and let her legs, impossibly heavy, sink to the cushioned mattress. She felt the hint of an ache in untried muscles but even that felt satisfying. Her arms clasped Raul tight. She could barely breathe but the feel of him blanketing her was…comforting.

Stunned, she thought about opening her eyes, but the notion of reality intruding on the single most remarkable experience of her life stopped her.

Even now she couldn't put a name to the feelings that had burst out of nowhere when she'd confronted Raul at their wedding reception. Or when he'd dared her to make love with him. No…have sex with him.

She swallowed, trying to ignore the strange winded sensation in the region of her heart.

If that was having sex, what would making love be like?

How could something so glorious have come out of such turbulent emotions?

Luisa waited for shame to engulf her. For regret that she'd given herself to a man who, though her husband, didn't truly care for her, didn't love her.

Yes, there was regret. Sadness that she'd never know what it was like to be with a man she loved and who loved her.

Yet she couldn't hide from the fact that with Raul she'd felt...different, glorious, powerful. The words didn't do justice to the sensation of soaring, of life and excitement and pleasure bubbling through her veins when they'd come together. Even when they argued it was there, a hidden promise that egged her on to defy him.

What did it mean? Luisa's brow knotted as she tried to work through her feelings. But she was too dazed by the enormity of what had just happened. Thinking was too hard when simply lying here with Raul was so wonderful.

A knuckle gently grazed her brow. 'Don't frown. It's not the end of the world.'

Luisa's eyes snapped open and she found herself staring into Raul's face. He looked as perplexed as she felt. A lock of dark hair tumbled over his brow, making him seem younger, more approachable. Her hand itched to brush it from his forehead but, despite what they'd just shared, the act seemed too intimate.

He moved, easing his weight onto his elbow, and she flushed, realising they were still joined intimately. She looked away but he turned her head towards him.

'You didn't tell me.'

'Tell you what?' The lovely lax feeling of contentment vanished and her muscles tensed.

'That you hadn't done this before.' His beautiful mouth twisted.

Had it been that obvious? While the passion lasted it hadn't mattered to Luisa. All that counted was her need and the fact that Raul reciprocated with equal urgency. Had he been disappointed? Her stomach dived.

'Does it matter?' She kept her gaze fixed on his mouth rather than his knowing eyes.

His lips thinned. 'Of course it mattered. I would have made sure it was better for you.'

Her gaze flew up, colliding with an intense green stare. It was on the tip of her tongue to ask how it could possibly be better, but she managed to stop herself.

At the memory of what they'd done Luisa breathed deep, internal muscles clenching. To her shock she felt an answering throb inside as Raul stirred. His mouth tipped into a smile that was rueful and devastatingly glorious and Luisa's heartbeat picked up speed.

'I could do that now,' he offered. To her amazement, Luisa felt her body hum with answering desire. So soon!

It frightened her how easily he'd made her need him. How readily she responded. Despite his occasional devastating tenderness, to him she was a convenience.

If she tried she'd convince herself what they'd just done meant as little to her as it must to him.

She just had to try harder.

'I need to get up. This dress will be a mess.'

Abruptly he withdrew, his smile fading. Luisa bit her tongue rather than cry out for him not to move. Without his weight pressing on her she felt lost.

How could she miss his touch so soon?

Shakily she drew her crumpled skirts down over her nakedness while he stood and adjusted his trousers. She had to remember he was used to dealing with desire. With sex. For him it was nothing special.

'Here, let me.' He took her arm and drew her up to a sitting position.

Avoiding his eyes, Luisa looked down at her

creased and rumpled silk. Her throat clogged. 'It's ruined.'

'Nonsense. It just needs a little attention. Don't worry, the palace has expert launderers.'

Shakily Luisa stroked the fabric, noticing a tear in the fine lace, feeling dampness at her bodice where Raul had suckled. What had seemed magnificent just minutes ago now seemed anything but. 'They'll know what we've done.'

'No one expects us to be celibate.' Once more he tilted her chin up. 'You shouldn't be ashamed of what we did.' He paused and she sensed he hesitated. 'Are you?'

Something passed between them, a surge of heat, a sense memory of passion. Luisa felt fire flicker in her belly. So, it wasn't over after all. It was still there, this…craving for his touch.

That was when she faced the truth. 'No, I'm not ashamed.' She wanted her husband still, again.

She shouldn't crave intimacy with the man who'd treated her so. Yet the feelings he unleashed subverted her pride.

'Good. Because I intend for it to happen often.' His hand slipped up to caress her cheek and she caught her breath at the gleaming promise in his look. 'Turn around and I'll help you out of that dress. You'll feel better after a bath.'

Luisa twisted sideways, telling herself she wasn't disappointed at his prosaic request.

It was only natural she'd enjoy sex with her virile, handsome husband. They were young and healthy. These…urges were to be expected. Yet she couldn't shake the feeling that nothing was quite that simple.

Luisa didn't understand her feelings. One minute he outraged her. The next he intrigued. He wasn't the sort of man she told herself she wanted, yet there were times when she liked him too much.

Perhaps she'd fallen for his expert seduction? He was vastly experienced and she a complete novice. Yet there'd been precious little seduction. He'd seemed as out of control as she. Luisa recalled the dazed look in his eyes and how he'd gasped an apology because he hadn't been able to hold back. As if she'd wanted him to!

Her lips curved and her thighs squeezed as satisfaction curled within her.

'Hold still while I get this veil.' The feel of his hands fumbling in her hair sent rivulets of heat through her. Finally he drew the veil aside and tossed it onto a plush chair, a stream of heirloom lace. A reminder, if she needed one, that they came from separate worlds. She couldn't imagine treating such a work of art so cavalierly.

Then she remembered how she'd thrown herself at him, heedless of the beautiful things she wore.

He brought out a side to her she didn't know.

The touch of Raul's fingers at her nape made her breath catch as the mattress dipped behind her.

'This will take a while.' The couturier had insisted on a myriad of buttons, each with its own tiny loop.

Raul sat close, his breath feathering her bare skin. She straightened, nipples tingling. In the silence she heard her breathing grow shallow.

'I wondered...'

'Yes?' She'd never heard Raul hesitant.

'Why were you so set against coming here? It wasn't just the prospect of marriage. From the first you were negative, instantly opposed to inheriting.'

'It bothers you that I didn't swoon at your feet?' Yet from the first Raul had got under her skin as no other.

'If I ever expected that, I know better now. Besides, I prefer you as you are.' Instead of annoyance, she thought she heard admiration in his voice.

Did her senses conspire to fool her?

His fingers brushed her back and her flesh drew tight. A coiling pulse began low in her belly. He devastated her defences. Luisa drew a sharp breath, seeking control.

'Won't you tell me?' His voice was a dark velvet caress.

She shut her eyes. What would it hurt?

'When I was sixteen my mother was diagnosed with a terminal illness. I looked after her.'

'I'm sorry. That must have been hard.'

She nodded, her throat tight. 'At least I was with her. But the point is, just before that some strangers came to the farm, wanting to talk to me. They were sent by my grandfather.' Even now she had to force that word out. The man didn't deserve the title.

'Not to see your mother?'

'No.' A sour taste flooded her mouth. 'His offer was for me alone. He invited me to live with him and learn to be a real princess.' She paused, clasping unsteady hands as she recalled the grandiose promises and the demands.

'At first I was excited. I was thrilled to see him, to be in his home. It was like a fairy tale. Even though he kept me busy at the palace, training me, he said, for when I'd be ready to take my proper place with him.'

'You actually came here? I didn't know.'

She nodded. 'No one did. Obviously I wasn't up

to his high standards. But I was here long enough to get his measure and that of the people he mixed with. That put me off ever returning.' She laughed hollowly. 'I was naïve. It took a while to realise I was just a puppet to manipulate. No choices. No career. No control over my own destiny.'

The skimming touch of Raul's fingers was gentle, almost a caress. She knew a ridiculous desire to sink back against him.

'When news came of my mother's illness I saw him for what he really was. He insisted I sever all links with my parents. He hated that my mother had walked out on the life he'd planned for her—a duty wife to some crony. He never forgave her. When I begged for help to get her better care, he was furious. According to him, she'd ceased to exist the moment she'd left her home.'

Luisa shuddered as she recalled the old man's vitriol. His cruelty.

'By marrying a commoner she'd diluted her aristocratic bloodlines. It was only his extreme generosity that enabled him to overlook my tainted birth and offer to take me in.'

A stream of low-voiced Maritzian cut the air. No mistaking its furious, violent edge.

'I knew he was old-fashioned.' Raul's voice was a lethal whisper. 'But that's just vicious.'

Luisa felt tears prickle, hearing his outrage and sympathy. It wrapped round her like a warm blanket.

She'd never told her parents. Couldn't bear to repeat it, though she suspected her mum had guessed some of it.

Relief filled her at finally spilling the awful truth.

'So you went back to the farm.'

'Mum needed me. And so did Dad. When she died it almost broke him.'

'Which is when you started taking responsibility for the co-op. I'm sorry, Luisa.'

She stiffened. 'There's nothing to be sorry for. I *wanted* to be with them.'

'I meant I'm sorry your first contact with Maritz was so poisonous. No wonder you hated the idea of the place.'

Her laugh was bitter. 'You can say that again. I thought the place full of the worst sort of people.'

'Not just your grandfather?'

She hesitated, aware she'd again strayed into territory she'd never shared.

'Luisa?' He paused. 'Do you want to tell me?' It was the concern in his tone that did it. The gentleness.

'There was a guy a little older than me at my grandfather's palace.' She sucked in a breath. 'No one knew I was the prince's granddaughter but when we met in the gardens it didn't seem to matter who I was. We talked and talked.' She cut herself off. How gullible she'd been!

'We met daily. And I…fell for him.' He'd kissed her and she'd believed herself in love. 'He wanted to elope but I refused.' She'd wanted her parents at her wedding.

'That upset him. He tried…' Foul memories surged, chilling her to the marrow and she was grateful for Raul's warmth. 'He tried to force me but I fought him. He left with a black eye, but not before he'd explained the reason he'd bothered with me was because of who I was. He'd found out and decided to use that to his advantage. He was ambitious, you see. Marrying a princess would be a coup.'

'Luisa—' Raul's deep voice was gruff '—I'm sorry.'

'It's not your fault.'

'But it's my country, my people.' No mistaking his regret and indignation.

A touch feathered between her shoulder blades as if he'd pressed his lips there. She was so tempted to ask him to love her again till the disturbing memories receded and all she knew was ecstasy.

Raul made her needy. He made her want things she shouldn't.

On wobbly legs she stood, clasping the loose dress close. She needed to take control. She'd already revealed enough. Despite the relief of sharing, she felt raw.

'I can manage now, if you point me to the bathroom.'

'Let me help.' From behind he tugged the dress.

Resisting would tear the fabric so she cooperated, only to find her bra had somehow got caught up with the gown. Hurriedly she crossed her arms over bare breasts.

'That's enough. I—'

He dragged the cloth down till it pooled at her feet.

Too late she remembered her panties lay in shreds somewhere. She clamped a hand between her legs, feeling moisture there, a reminder of the sex they'd shared. There wasn't even a robe or a towel to cover her nakedness.

He circled before her, tall in his exquisite finery while she wore nothing but stay-up stockings. She felt vulnerable, especially before his magnificent height.

'You're stunning.' The thickening timbre of his voice splintered her thoughts. 'Let me look at you.'

The avid glitter in his eyes, the way his nostrils flared as if to drag in oxygen, spoke of a man at the edge of control. She felt his hands tremble as he took hers. He swallowed jerkily and tendons stood out in his neck.

She'd never been naked before a man. Embarrassed heat flushed her skin. But with it came a buzz of excitement, a rising sense of power.

For Raul looked...enthralled.

Again he swallowed and she saw the rapid pulse in his throat. It mirrored her heartbeat.

He looked like a starving man before a feast, not sure where to begin. She felt again that stirring of power.

With a visible effort he dragged his gaze up. His eyes had a strange unfocused look. Slowly he shook his head. He released her and stepped back.

'You were a virgin. You'll be sore. I shouldn't...'

She didn't feel sore. Not much. She felt wonderful. Because he wanted her as she wanted him? Or because he cared enough to hold back? To put her needs first.

She hugged the knowledge close. It was a small thing but it felt significant.

When he gently scooped her in his arms Luisa curled into him. She delighted in the steady thump of his heart as he carried her to the bathroom.

Minutes later she sank back with a sigh in warm scented water. It was bliss on the gentle ache of muscles.

Under lowered lashes she watched Raul strip off his jacket, roll up the sleeves of his collarless shirt and reach for a large sponge. Anticipation zinged through her.

His swirling touch with the sponge was impossibly erotic. She gripped the massive tub rather than reach up to brush back the dark lock tumbling over his forehead. He tended her so gently. As if she were precious.

Sweat sheened his face. It trickled down his throat and she wanted to slide her hand along his skin. But his taut frown and grim mouth deterred her.

Until she noticed the bulge in his trousers. No wonder he looked in pain. No wonder his big capable hands shook so badly he'd dropped the soap more than once.

The knowledge set every nerve ablaze.

'I'm getting out.' Luisa struggled to rise.

'Wait!' Heedless of the water, Raul hauled her out with an ease that reminded her of the power hidden under his clothes. She sank into him, spreading her hands over his saturated shirt and muscled chest.

'You need rest.' His jaw set hard as if with strain.

'That's not what I need.' She tilted her chin and met his gaze. 'I need you.'

There, she'd said it and the world hadn't collapsed around her! In fact it felt good.

'Now.' Her fingers curled tight in his sodden shirt. She raised herself on tiptoe and pressed her lips to his.

In a flurry of urgent movement he lifted her, strode out and laid her on the bed. Seconds later he'd ripped his shirt open and shrugged it off. Luisa's pulse rocketed as she took in his sculpted torso with its smattering of dark hair. His hands went to his trousers as he heeled off his shoes. A moment later he stood naked and imposing.

She forgot to breathe as she surveyed his perfect form, felt the power radiating from him. Then thought ended as he joined her. He was like a furnace, burning hot.

He touched her all over, palms smooth, fingers teasing. He skimmed and stroked and even tickled till she squirmed and tried to reciprocate. But he held her, his thigh clamped her still, his hands capturing her wrists.

The torture began as he used his lips, tongue and teeth on her body. Minutes turned into an aeon of pleasure.

It was as if he tried to compensate for the speed

of their earlier coupling. Delight piled upon delight till Luisa was strung out, quivering with need and pleasure. It was too much, too intense.

'Please, Raul,' she gasped. 'Don't tease.'

He looked up under hooded lids and her breath snagged as he tugged with his mouth at her breast. He held her gaze as his tongue circled her nipple then lapped hard, drawing hot wires of desire through her taut body. She groaned and instantly his hand slid down, stroking at her most sensitive point.

That was all it took.

She cried out as waves of ecstasy crested and crashed within her. Still he held her gaze, even as the world swirled around her and she bucked helplessly beneath his touch. It was wonderful; it left her speechless.

But it wasn't *Raul*.

Luisa clutched at his shoulders and finally, as she sagged spent against the mattress, he settled between her thighs. The feel of his hot flesh there sent a spark of energy through her lax bones and a searing sense of familiarity. Of rightness.

This time he slid home easily. She rejoiced in each magnificent centimetre, excitement stirring anew as he propped his weight above her. His solid chest brushed her sensitive nipples. Friction built to combustible levels with each measured thrust.

But it was his eyes that transfixed her. The connection between them was different this time. She read arousal and restraint in his gaze. And more. Something unguarded and raw. Something honest.

Raul moved faster and Luisa tilted her hips to meet him. Pleasure coiled tighter, lashing them together. It reached breaking point and still their eyes locked.

The climax came. Earth-shattering, mind-blowing ecstasy that went on and on. Through it all their gazes held in silent communication.

It felt like they shared as equals.

CHAPTER NINE

REALITY hit when Luisa woke.

Last night she'd almost believed they shared more than their bodies. But waking alone in Raul's bed reminded her where his priorities lay. Their marriage was about his desire for power. Sex was a bonus they shared.

Her chest tightened as she forced herself to think of it as sex. *It had felt like making love.*

Yet he'd left it to a maid to wake his bride, discreetly pretending not to notice the rumpled bed or that Luisa was naked beneath the fine linen.

Fire scorched Luisa's skin as the girl swept up the rumpled wedding gown, folding the metres of fine hand-worked veil with the reverence it deserved.

Memories seared, of Raul flinging the veil away. Of her standing with the dress at her feet as he held her arms wide and feasted on the sight of her. Of their blazing passion, utterly heedless of her exquisite finery.

Thrumming arousal beat low in her body, just remembering. Appalled, Luisa realised the need

Raul had awoken was far from sated. How much she'd changed in one night!

She nodded vaguely as the maid, eyes carefully averted, pointed out the door in the panelling connecting to Luisa's room, for when she wanted to dress.

Luisa hadn't known the apartments were connected. She hadn't even recognised the corridor when Raul had brought her here! She'd been so caught up in her response to him.

Alone at last, Luisa stared at the empty pillow beside her.

She had no right to feel disappointed. She'd known what she was doing. She'd initiated it! But through a night of intimacy, curled close in his arms, she'd forgotten.

What they'd shared had been purely physical. Her skin prickled as she recalled how eager she'd been. It had been almost a relief to let anger push her into reckless desire.

She'd given herself, *knowing* where she fitted in his world. Raul viewed her in terms of her usefulness to him. Despite his tenderness, in that he was like her grandfather.

Pain cramped her belly. Her dream of one day finding love like her parents was dead. This—the ecstasy and the loneliness—would be her lot.

Maybe that was why she'd imagined the fragile connection between them: because it was easier than facing reality.

But she couldn't hide from the world for ever.

Ignoring the breakfast tray, Luisa wrapped a sheet around herself and hurried to the connecting door, determined not to yield to weak regrets. She'd made her bed and now...

She grabbed the door frame and braced herself as sudden realisation smote her. Her knees shook so hard she feared she'd slide to the floor.

They hadn't used contraception! How could she only just have realised?

It scared her—how much Raul scrambled her thoughts. How she changed when she was with him. He raised passions she'd never known. Her every emotion, from anger to joy, seemed so much more intense because of him.

Giving herself to him surely made her more vulnerable to his potent influence. But it was too late to turn back.

All she could do was try to be sensible, remembering they shared a pragmatic, convenient relationship. She couldn't afford to fall into the trap of foolish dreams.

She'd begin with contraception. She wasn't ready to bring a baby into such a situation.

* * *

'Your Highnesses, welcome.' The mayor bowed low, his bald head gleaming in the sun.

But Raul's attention wasn't on the resplendent figure before the town hall. It was riveted on Luisa. In her pale suit and with her golden hair swept up she looked coolly elegant. Yet a darting glance at her full lips and the slenderness of her throat brought waves of memory crashing in on him.

Of Luisa beneath him last night, writhing with a desperate pleasure tinged by innocent wonder that had held him in thrall despite his urgent need for completion. Of her unrestrained passion that blasted through his sophistication and years of experience and reduced him to slavering, uncontrolled need.

As if *he* was the virgin and she the seducer!

Even the feel of her arm as he guided her over the uneven cobblestones made hunger spring to gnawing life. He had to call on all his experience to mask his feelings.

That was what worried him. The fact that she made him *feel*. Not merely mind-blowing lust. Nor simply relief and gratitude that the crown was assured.

A cocktail of emotions had stirred last night as she'd spoken of her grandfather and her would-be seducer. A fierce protectiveness utterly unlike that he felt for his country. Fury at her hurts. Sadness. Tenderness he'd never known.

And joy so profound it had shocked him to the core and driven him from bed this morning, seeking work as a distraction.

Instinctively he tried to deny the intensity of his emotions. He didn't do feelings. That was how he'd survived and rebuilt his life in the face of humiliating public speculation and private pain.

What did Luisa do to him?

Even as a youth, when he'd been smitten by what he'd foolishly deemed love, he'd functioned better than this.

The crowd cheered and it was all Raul could do to remember to wave in acknowledgement. For the first time he had difficulty remembering his duty.

The realisation terrified him.

Duty had been his life. He'd devoted himself to his country with a dedication other men gave to wives and families. It gave him purpose. Had kept him going in that bleak time when his world crashed around him.

'Prince Raul, Princess Luisa, welcome.' The mayor's eyes gleamed admiringly as he bowed to Luisa.

Raul tensed at his blatant stare. He knew an unreasoning desire to pull Luisa behind him out of sight. Or take her to the castle and lock her in his bedroom.

Now *there* was a thought!

The crisp wind brought colour to her cheeks. Last night's passion had softened her lips to a lush, inviting bow that played havoc with his self-control and sent blood surging to his groin. Any minute now and the snapping cameras would catch him in rampant arousal.

'Your Highness?'

A look at the mayor's puzzled face told Raul they were waiting for him.

Dredging up his control, Raul spoke, finding calm in the give and take of official welcome. Yet the undercurrent of awareness heightening every sense disturbed him. A night of passion should slake desire, not increase it.

The mayor turned to Luisa, holding out a huge ornamental key that signified her free entry to every locked building in the capital.

'Welcome to our city, Your Highness. I hope you will be as happy here with us as we are to have you among us.' He spoke in Maritzian then English and the crowd cheered.

She looked sexy as hell. No trace now of the androgynous mud-spattered farmer. Raul imagined unbuttoning her jacket as he'd undone her wedding gown last night and—

'Thank you so much. It's a pleasure to be here.' To Raul's amazement Luisa spoke in slow but clear Maritzian as she turned towards the people lining the square. 'It's kind of you all to come and welcome me to your lovely city. I'll look forward to discovering it for myself.'

The crowd roared.

It didn't matter that Luisa had turned from the microphone so the sound blurred, or that her accent wasn't perfect. The fact that she made the effort to speak Maritzian, when everyone knew from the press release that she wasn't fluent, endeared her to them.

The mayor beamed. Streamers waved and a ripple of applause rose.

Pride surged as Raul watched her smile at the throng. Only he, beside her, saw the stiff set of her jaw and how her hands shook as she clasped the heavy key.

Only he, the man who'd forced her into leaving everything she knew and adopting a role she'd rejected time and again, guessed what it cost her to put on this façade.

Razor-sharp pain speared through him. He'd

done what he must for his nation and Luisa had been the one to suffer.

A memory flashed of her pain last night as she'd spoken of her grandfather's manipulation. Raul's hands balled to fists. His own demands must have been like an echo of that dreadful time. The knowledge stirred an uncomfortable, unfamiliar sensation. *Guilt.*

He'd plucked her from her world, one where she was loved and appreciated, and dropped her into an alien place. Into a role even those born to it found challenging.

Last night they'd shared physical pleasure. But he'd persuaded and challenged her into it. Would she have come to him of her own volition?

'Here, let me.' He took the key, disturbed at the shame he felt. He wasn't used to questioning his actions. He'd spent so long sure in the knowledge he acted for the public good.

'It's almost over,' he murmured. 'Just back to the car and that's it.'

Finally Luisa met his eyes and shock sucker-punched him. Gone was the wonderment and warmth that, despite his attempts to rationalise, had turned last night into something remarkable. Something he refused to analyse.

For the first time since she'd agreed to marry, Luisa's gaze was coolly remote.

Inexplicable loss filled him. He'd thought they'd begun to share something more than an acceptance of duty. Instinctively Raul reached for her but she moved away.

At the last moment he remembered to thank the mayor. By the time he'd finished Luisa was ahead of him, her spine erect and poise perfect. That hadn't been learned in the last week. Her mother's teaching?

He followed, his gaze drawn to the slim skirt that shifted over her curves with every step. That was why he didn't see the bustle on the edge of the crowd. The next thing he knew, one of the security staff lunged across the open space while another hurried forward. Instantly alert, Raul raced across the cobbles, adrenalin pumping, ready to protect her.

He skidded to a halt beside her as she bent. That was when he saw the ragamuffin dog, all hair and lolling tongue, gambolling at her feet.

Raul's heart crashed against his ribs. When he'd seen the security men swing into action he'd feared the worst. If anything had happened to her...

'Luisa, he's filthy.' The words were brusque,

sharper than he'd intended as relief flared. His wife gave him a wide-eyed stare.

His wife! The world shifted beneath his feet and Raul couldn't tell if it was from shock or reaction to the reproach in her eyes.

'He's just a harmless puppy.' She cradled the mongrel, looking down and murmuring in a soft tone that made the beast wriggle in ecstasy.

If Luisa smiled at him that way, whispering and rubbing his belly, Raul would lap it up too. His groin tightened. Damn it! This was ridiculous. She only had to smile and he got as hard as a randy teenager. He didn't understand it.

A commotion caught his eye. A small boy was trying to get past Raul's staff. Raul nodded to them to let him pass.

The kid cast a fearful glance over his shoulder then hurried forward. Raul saw a scowling red-faced man in the crowd where the boy had been.

For an instant memory side-swiped Raul. Of his own father wearing that same expression on one of the few occasions he'd deigned to spend time with his young son. Raul couldn't remember what he'd done to earn his father's wrath. Scuffed his shoes perhaps or earned a less than perfect mark in his studies. It hadn't taken much to disappoint the old man.

Bitterness welled on his tongue and his eyes narrowed.

The boy stopped before them, his head sinking low.

'Is this your dog?' Raul had to wait for a silent nod and felt Luisa's hand on his arm.

What? Did she think he'd rip into the kid?

'Yes, sir. He means no harm, sir. The cord broke and—'

'Completely understandable,' Raul said. 'With all that noise it's not surprising he got overexcited.'

The boy raised his head and stared, as if unable to believe his ears.

'He must have sensed the Princess likes dogs.' Raul found himself talking just to reassure. He'd had no idea Luisa liked dogs till he saw her cuddle this one. She smiled at the boy and crouched down to his level.

Good with children and dogs. Raul watched the boy's nervousness disappear under the warmth of Luisa's approval and realised she was a natural with both. She'd make a great mother—warm and affectionate. He watched her hand the pup over and pat the kid reassuringly.

Raul could imagine her with an unruly brood, unfazed by soccer in the gloomy royal portrait gallery on a wet winter's day or kids who wanted to run outdoors instead of perfecting their Latin before they were allowed dinner.

Something scooped a hollow deep in Raul's belly at the thought of Luisa with children. *They'd be his children.*

For the first time the idea of fatherhood appealed, even though he had no experience of real family life.

He tried to imagine Luisa carrying his child and found the notion strangely satisfying. Though not as pleasurable as having her to himself, naked and needy.

'It's time to go.' He took her arm and helped her rise. Then he steered his wife and the boy towards the beet-faced man at the front of the crowd.

He wanted his wife to himself, had wanted her since he'd forced himself to leave her this morning. But first he had business to attend to.

Luisa raised a hand to wave at the crowd pressed close to the road. Safer to look at them than the man beside her who continually bewildered her.

Self-conscious, she crossed her legs over the ladder creeping up her stockings where the pup had scratched. Then she wiped at the muddy stains on her designer suit.

'Don't fidget with your clothes. No one else can see the dirt.'

Startled, she turned. She'd thought Raul focused on the crowd on the other side of the road. Even now he didn't turn. She had a perfect view of his austere profile as he waved. Luisa found her gaze lingering on his full lower lip as she remembered the way he'd kissed her last night.

Heat spiralled inside and she swallowed hard. It didn't do any good. She couldn't quench the need he'd ignited.

Obviously Raul wasn't similarly bothered. He was utterly composed. No doubt displeased by her behaviour in picking up a grubby little dog that was anything but pedigree. Her eyes shut as she imagined the press pictures. Raul looking regal and she with a ladder in her stockings.

Well, tough! She hadn't asked to be princess. He'd stampeded her into it. Now he could put up with the fact that she didn't fit the mould.

She'd read his stern demeanour through the ceremony today. As if waiting for her to embarrass herself. Not even her carefully rehearsed lines, learned with Lukas' help, had softened Raul's severe countenance.

Had she really sought his approval? The notion of such neediness disturbed her.

Only once in the whole proceedings had his face softened. With the boy.

'Why did we go over to that man in the crowd?' She hadn't even been aware of the question forming in her head.

Raul turned and a sizzle shot through her as their gazes collided.

Luisa slumped back against her seat, heart pounding as fire roared through her veins. How did he do that? Was it the same for all the women he bedded?

The idea was pure torture.

'I wanted to make sure there was no trouble.'

'Trouble?' Luisa scrabbled for coherent thought.

'He was complaining loudly about his son being uncontrollable. And about what a nuisance the dog was.'

'You're kidding!' Luisa straightened. 'Peter was a darling, but so serious, not uncontrollable. If anything he seemed too old for his years.' She hadn't understood everything he'd said but his gravity had struck her.

Raul shrugged but the movement seemed cramped. 'Living with a judgemental parent will do that.'

It was on the tip of Luisa's tongue to question Raul's assessment, till she read a bleakness in his eyes that made her back off.

'What did you say to his father?' Raul had looked every inch the monarch, full of gracious condescension.

Again that shrug. A little easier this time. 'I congratulated him on his fine son.'

'Good on you!'

Startled green eyes met hers and for a moment Luisa lost the thread of the conversation.

'And I invited both boy and dog to visit the castle, to renew the acquaintance.'

Luisa tried but couldn't read Raul's expression. Yet instinct told her why he'd done it. 'You wanted to make sure he didn't get rid of the pup?'

For an instant longer Raul held her gaze before turning back to the window and raising his hand in acknowledgement of the people thronging the road.

'A boy should be allowed a dog for companionship. Don't you think?'

His tone indicated the matter was of no importance. Yet she remembered Peter's trembling fear and the nervous way he'd eyed his father. Raul had gone out of his way to speak to them when he hadn't made time to glad-hand anyone else in the crowd, preferring to wave from a distance.

Luisa sensed the matter was anything but unimportant to Raul. The scenario had struck a chord with him.

Frowning, she realised she knew almost nothing about the man she'd married.

CHAPTER TEN

R<small>AUL</small>'S mother had died in childbirth, his father had been impatient with children and Raul didn't have siblings. That was all Luisa knew, apart from the fact that he distanced himself behind a formidable reserve.

What did that say about him?

'Did you have a dog when you were a boy?'

Raul shot her a surprised look as they drove through the castle gates.

'No,' he said finally, his expression unreadable. 'Dogs and antique heirlooms aren't a good mix.'

Luisa surveyed the enormous courtyard and thought of the labyrinth of terraces, walled gardens and moats around the castle. 'There's room enough outside.'

If *she* had a child she'd let him or her have a pet or three and find a way to protect the antiques.

Shock grabbed her throat as she realised she was imagining a sturdy little boy running across the courtyard with black hair and eyes as green as emeralds. Eyes like—

'Are you ready, Luisa?' She looked up to find Raul already standing beside the limousine, offering his hand. No way to avoid touching him without being pointedly rude. Yet, even braced for it, the shock that sparked from his touch and ran up her arm stunned her.

Raul gave no sign of anything untoward, which left her wondering again if it were she alone overreacting to last night's intimacy. Sternly she told herself it was natural she'd respond to the touch of her first ever lover. But when he tucked her arm through his and led her through the cavernous entrance, it was all she could do to repress the shivers of excitement running through her body. Being this close set desire humming through her.

'Who did you play with?' She sought distraction.

One dark brow winged up towards Raul's hairline, giving him a faintly dangerous air.

'I had little time for play. Princes may be born but they need to be moulded for the role too.'

Luisa stared, horrified. But his cool tone signalled an end to the subject and he picked up his pace, leading her swiftly towards the lift.

'But when you were little you must have played.'

He shrugged, the movement brushing his arm against her. She breathed in the subtle scent of warm male skin.

'I don't recall. I had tutors and lessons from the age of four. Playtime wasn't scheduled, though later sports were included in the curriculum.'

'That sounds…regimented.' She smothered her outrage and distress. Surely they could have allowed him some time to be a child! It reinforced her resolve not to risk having a baby. No child of hers would be treated so.

Raul punched the button for the lift. 'My days were busy.'

Busy, not happy. The ancient castle was perfect for hide and seek and the fantasy games young children revelled in. Had he ever played them? Her heart went out to the little boy he'd been, so lonely, she suspected now.

Did that loneliness explain his aloof attitude? His formidable self-possession?

'Did you see much of your father?' She recalled him saying his father had been impatient with children. How had that impacted? She had no idea how royal households worked but she guessed no man became as ferociously self-sufficient as Raul without reason.

Her husband shot a warning look that shivered her skin. Luisa looked straight back.

The lift rose smoothly, so smoothly she knew it hadn't caused the dropping sensation in her stomach that came with the word *husband*.

'My father was busy. He had a country to run.'

Luisa bit down hard rather than blurt out her sympathy. The doors slid open but Luisa didn't move.

'Do you mean he didn't have time for you?'

She could almost see the shutters come down over Raul's face, blanking out all expression. The suddenness of it chilled her. Yet, far from blanking her out, it made her want to wrap her arms around him. The image of Peter, the little boy in the market square, so quaintly formal, tugged at her heart. Had Raul been like that as a child?

Her own glorious childhood, filled with laughter and love, happy days on the river or riding the tractor with her dad, running riot with a couple of dogs and even a pet lizard were halcyon by comparison.

'Why do you want to know?'

'Why don't you want to tell me? I'm your wife.' She didn't even stumble over the word. 'It's right I know you better.' Yet it was like pulling teeth, trying to get him to open up even a little.

Raul stood still, his face taut and unreadable. Then she caught a flicker in his eyes that made her thighs quiver and her stomach tighten.

'Just what I had in mind.' His voice lowered to a deep resonance that caressed her skin. 'Getting to know each other better.' Raul tugged her into the carpeted hallway and she realised they stood in front of his suite.

The glint in his eyes was unmistakable. Desire, raw and hungry. Something feral and dangerous sent delicious excitement skimming through her.

Her eyes widened. No mistaking what he meant. Sex.

It was in his knowing look. In the deep shuddering breath that expanded his wide chest, as if he had trouble filling oxygen starved lungs.

Luisa waited for outrage to take hold. For pride to give her the strength to shove him away. Indignation didn't come. It was excitement that knotted her stomach. Desire that clogged her throat.

He'd introduced her to pleasure and she was too inexperienced to hide the fact that she craved more.

Raul must have read her feelings for his lips curved in a smile that made her pulse jitter. Wordlessly he shoved open the door, pulled her in and against him as he leaned back, closing the door with his body.

Fire exploded in her blood. Last night she'd loved the heavy burden of him above her. Now she wanted to arch into him and revel in the hard solidity of his big frame. It was weak of her but she couldn't get enough of him.

She shoved aside the memory of this morning's

desolation, and the suspicion that his desire now masked a determination to stop her prying into his past.

At this moment it was Raul's passion she wanted. Perhaps because of the emptiness she'd glimpsed in his eyes when he'd spoken so casually about a childhood that to her sounded frighteningly cold. Did she doom herself to a similar loneliness, marrying him?

Yet it wasn't fear that drove her. Or simple lust.

Her heart twisted as she realised she wanted to give herself to her husband in the hope of healing some of the deep hurt she'd seen flicker for a moment in his eyes.

'Luisa? Do you want this?'

'Yes.' She didn't try to hide from his searching gaze.

When he lowered his head to graze the side of her neck with his teeth the air sucked straight out of her lungs. Thought disintegrated as she sank into pleasure.

She opened her eyes and groaned as he bit into the sensitive flesh at the base of her throat. Her hands clenched at his shoulders as his hands skimmed her jacket, undoing it and her shirt and spreading the open sides wide.

'You were magnificent this morning.' His voice was a low, throaty purr as he stripped off her jacket then kissed the upper slope of her breasts as he shoved her blouse off. Her skirt followed moments later and she shivered in sensual delight as he ran his big hands over her hips.

'I just did what was expected.' Yet she felt a tiny burst of pleasure at his words. Having accepted her new role, she was determined to do it well.

She sighed as he fastened his mouth on her lacy bra, sucking hard till the nipple stood erect and darts of liquid fire shot to her core.

Convulsively she shuddered, cradling him close, overwhelmed by the sudden need to embrace him and comfort him. This big man who needed no one.

He lifted his head and met her eyes. His own were shadowed, as if he veiled his thoughts. The knowledge pained her. He worked so hard to maintain his distance. Had he never learned to share anything? Was she crazy to think they could make this work?

Then his mouth descended and he swung her up in his embrace. Heat surrounded her. Hard-packed muscle. The steady beat of his heart.

By the time he lowered her to the bed and stripped both their clothes with a deftness that spoke of practice and urgency, Luisa's thoughts had almost scrambled.

'Contraception!' she blurted out as she sank beneath him. 'I don't want to get pregnant.'

His brows rose. 'We're married, Luisa. Having a child is a natural outcome.'

She shook her head. Despite the wonderful weighted feeling of his lower body on hers, this was too important.

'No. I'm not ready.' She gulped down air and tried to order her thoughts. 'It's been too fast.'

For what seemed an eternity Raul stared, as if seeing her for the first time. Finally he nodded and rolled away, reaching for the bedside table.

When he turned back he didn't immediately cover her body with his.

For a man who'd married her out of necessity he had a way of making her feel the absolute focus of his world. As if nothing existed but her. His total concentration, the intensity of his gaze, the knowing, deliberately seductive touch of his hands on her body, were exhilarating.

Raul's gaze softened with each circling stroke and she felt something shift deep inside. She arched into his touch and her pulse pounded in her ears. When he leaned close his breath was an erotic caress of her sensitive ear lobe that sent sparks of heat showering through her.

'Come for me, Luisa.' His fingers delved and a

ripple of sensation caught her. 'Give yourself up to it.'

Gasping, she focused on him, feeling the dip and wheel of excitement while the intense connection sparked between them. His set face, his mouth, no longer smiling but stretched taut in concentration. The furrow on his brow, his eyes...

Out of nowhere the orgasm hit, jerking her body and stealing her breath. Heat flared under her skin as he dipped his head to take her mouth in a long, languorous kiss that somehow intensified the echoing spasms.

Spent at last, she sank back into the bed.

Now he'd come to her. Dreamily she smiled, her inner muscles pulsing in readiness. Despite her exhaustion, it was Raul she wanted. The hollow ache inside was proof of that.

He moved, but not as she'd expected. Shocked, she saw him settling himself low, nuzzling her inner thighs.

'No! I want—'

His kiss silenced her. She shouldn't want more after the ecstasy that still echoed through her, but the caress of Raul's tongue, his lips, sent need jolting through her.

That was only the beginning.

Dazed, Luisa gave herself up to new caresses,

new sensations that built one on the other till all she knew was Raul and the pleasure he wrought in her malleable, ever eager body. The taste of him was on her tongue, his scent in her nostrils as she grew attuned to his touch and the deep approving rumble of his voice.

Blindly she turned to him as finally he took her for himself, his rampant hardness a contrast to her lush satiation. She breathed deep, taking his shuddering, powerful body into hers as she seemed to absorb his essence into her pores.

Raul cried out and pleasure drenched her at the sound of her name in that raw needy voice. Instinctively she clutched him protectively close.

Raul lay completely spent, only enough strength in his body to pull Luisa close, her body sprawled over him.

He told himself the post-coital glow was always this intense, but he knew he lied. From the moment he'd bedded his wife he'd known the sex was different.

Why? His brain wouldn't leave the question alone.

Because she didn't meekly comply with his wishes? Because, despite agreeing to marry, she was still her own woman, not like the compliant lovers who gave whatever he wanted because of what he could provide in return?

With Luisa he had the thrilling, faintly disturbing sense that he held a precious gift in his arms.

She was far more than a warm body to sate his lust.

This was unknown territory. Or, if he were honest with himself, a little too like the feelings he'd discovered in his youth, when he'd believed in love. The thought should terrify him. He was well past believing in such things.

His lips quirked ruefully. That was why he'd seduced his wife as soon as they'd got back from the civic ceremony. Not just because he wanted her, but to stop himself puzzling over what she made him feel.

And to stop her questions. His hand clenched in the silk of her hair and she shifted delectably, soft flesh against his. Was it possible he'd used sex to avoid talking about his past? Even something as simple as his childhood?

Was he really such a coward?

His life was an open book. It had been pored over and dissected by the media for years. Yet the discomfort he'd felt answering Luisa's questions surprised him.

As did the unfamiliar need to open up to her. To share a little of himself.

He frowned. It was absurd. He didn't need a confessor or a confidante. There was no need for conversation. Yet deep down he knew he lied.

Perhaps because of the sense that he owed her for agreeing to marry?

Whatever the reason, when she shifted as if to move away, he slipped a restraining arm around the curve of her waist and cleared his throat.

'My father was interested in me only as heir to the throne.' His voice sounded husky. Raul told himself it was the aftermath of that stunning climax.

'That's awful.' Her words were murmured against his chest. She didn't look up. Somehow that made it easier.

He shrugged. 'Staff raised me. That's the way it's always been in the royal household. He dropped by just enough to remind me I had to excel to be ready to wear the crown one day.'

'And you wonder why I'm not ready for children!'

Shock smote him. He'd spoken blithely about the possibility of pregnancy, but the reality hadn't sunk in. Luisa, pregnant with his child...

'No child of ours would be raised like that.' Certainty firmed on the words.

'Really?'

Raul nodded. He'd spent years adhering to tradition as he fought to stabilise the monarchy and the nation, working behind the scenes as his father's focus narrowed to pleasing his capricious young wife. It had been Raul who'd tried to redress the damage after the fiasco with Ana.

But some traditions needed change.

'You have my word.'

He might not be a success as a father. Certainly his father's model of paternal love had been distant and unemotional. He thought of Peter, the boy with his dog. At least Raul knew what *not* to do. And Luisa would make up for his shortcomings. She'd be a natural.

He smiled, satisfied at the prospect.

'Tell me…' She hesitated.

'Yes?'

'Yesterday at the reception. Why did everyone watch you and your stepmother as if they expected a scene?'

Raul drew a heavy breath, satisfaction dissipating in an instant. But Luisa had a right to know. As she'd pointed out, she was his wife. Better to learn the facts from him than from some gossip sheet.

'Because they know I don't like her.' He stroked Luisa's hair then down her back, distracting himself just a little by the way she arched into his caress.

'Why not?' Luisa's question was a breath of sound. 'Why don't you like her?'

Raul clenched his jaw, forcing himself to answer.

'She pretended to marry him for love. He was proud and arrogant and he'd never been in love before, but he didn't deserve what he got.' Even though at first Raul had wished them both to the devil. He'd found no satisfaction seeing his father, weighed down by regret, dwindle into a shadow of the man he'd been.

'He was duped by a gold-digger half his age who wanted wealth and royal prestige. She spent most of her time with other men. His last years were hell.'

Even in his anger Raul felt a weight slide off his chest. He'd kept his views to himself so long, knowing an unguarded word would inflame the gossip and speculation he'd tried so hard to quash. The truth of his father's marriage had been guessed by many but never proven.

He'd worked tirelessly to protect his family's reputation, covering for his father as he grew erratic and less able to control his kingdom. Overcoming a desire to expose Ana for the witch she was. His country needed faith in the monarchy that kept it stable.

'There's more, isn't there? More you're not telling?'

Raul felt movement and looked down to see Luisa's bright eyes surveying him. She looked troubled.

Briefly he hesitated. But there was no point refusing to tell her. She could find out easily enough. He looked up at the wood-panelled ceiling, away from her searching gaze.

'I met Ana in my early twenties. She was my age but unlike any of the girls I knew. She wasn't aristocratic. She didn't simper or talk in platitudes. She didn't talk politics and she didn't care about court gossip.'

His lips twisted at the memory.

'She was a breath of fresh air. Vibrant, outspoken, fun. She wasn't afraid to get her hair messed riding in a convertible, or enjoy a picnic out in the open instead of dinner at a chic restaurant.' Or so it had seemed.

'I was smitten.' Raul halted, drawing a searing breath. It was the first time he'd admitted it. Strange how the memory seemed less shattering. Maybe because he saw his youthful folly clearly since he no longer believed in love.

'Oh, Raul!' No mistaking Luisa's distress. Or the tension in her body. The story wasn't a pretty one. Suddenly he wanted it over as quickly as possible.

'It turned out I was wrong about her. She seemed

fresh and innocent, uncomplicated and appealing. But she wasn't what she appeared.' His mouth twisted.

'I wasn't the only one taken in. I introduced her to my father and he fell for her with all the force of an old fool for a very beautiful, very clever young woman.'

Raul remembered those days vividly. Ana had played him, holding him at arm's length once she got his father in her sights. After all, what price a prince when a king was available, with a kingdom's wealth at his disposal?

'My father married her four months later.'

Raul had thought his world had ended. He'd retreated into duty, throwing himself into anything that would dull the pain of betrayal. It had become habit to direct all his passion, all his energies into his royal obligations.

It had worked. Over the years he'd dispensed with the need for emotional ties.

'Raul, I'm so sorry. That must have been soul-destroying.'

Luisa didn't know the half of it. But it had made him stronger. He was self-sufficient and glad of it.

So why did he feel stripped naked in a way that had nothing to do with his lack of clothes?

'Do you still…care for her?'

Blindly Raul turned towards Luisa's voice, finally focusing on her troubled gaze.

'Care?' He almost spat the word. 'For the woman who deceived me and incited my own father to betray me?' A laugh tore, savage and rough, from his throat. 'For the woman who made me a laughing stock? She damned near destroyed the monarchy with her scandalous behaviour. She did destroy my father's pride and honour with her affairs.'

Raul shook his head. 'I learned a valuable lesson from her. Never to trust. Never to be gullible again. Love is a trap for the unwary.'

It struck him that what had drawn him to Ana all those years ago was what attracted him to Luisa. Her innocence in a world of political machinations. Her directness and honesty. Her beauty. Except in Luisa it was real. In Ana it had been false, designed to snare.

Ana had come to this apartment one morning just months after her wedding. She'd worn sheer black lace and even sheerer audacity and she'd expected Raul to satisfy her as his father hadn't been able to.

Rancid distaste filled his mouth. It had taken him a long time to banish the taint of that memory, even though he'd spurned her, avoiding her whenever he could.

In the long run Ana had done him a favour. Never again would he fall for the fantasy of love.

Luisa reeled from the shocking truth. The harsh light in his eyes as he'd spoken of his stepmother made her shiver.

Or was that because of the revelation that he'd once loved Ana?

Did he love her still? Despite his vehement denial, it was clear she still evoked strong emotion in him.

Nausea rose, threatening to choke Luisa. Raul had taken her with the compulsion of a man staking his claim.

Or a man intent on obliterating the past.

Had he really wanted *her*? Or had his pent-up passion been for the woman who'd rejected him yet still had a place in his life? Was Luisa a stand-in?

She bit her lip.

He'd said he didn't believe in love. Had he already fallen so hard for Ana he couldn't escape his feelings?

And if not, why did the idea of Raul, deprived of love as a child and now rejecting it as an adult, fill Luisa with sadness?

CHAPTER ELEVEN

LUISA peeked through slitted eyes as Raul dressed. She'd fallen into an exhausted sleep despite the swirl of disturbing thoughts his revelations had produced.

Hours ago they'd scaled the heights of bliss and she'd felt absurdly as if she'd found the other half of her soul in his arms, especially when he'd then begun to open up a little about his life.

But his later revelations about Ana had poisoned that heady pleasure and made her doubt.

What did Raul feel? Would she ever know?

She swallowed a knot of distress. The best she could do for herself, and the man she feared she was coming to care too much for, was be sensible—take a day at a time and try to build a workable marriage.

Easier said than done when just looking at him made her heart clench.

Hair slicked back from the shower, strong hands knotting his tie, Raul looked more potently sexy than any man had a right to.

Was this how his other lovers felt when he left them? She breathed through the hurt.

There could never be love between them.

Raul had closed himself off from that possibility. His bitterness over his father's wife skewed his emotions so much he'd admitted he'd never trust a woman, or love, again.

Who could blame him, after the devastating betrayal he'd suffered? Pain seared her as she recalled the stoical way he'd revealed the bare bones of the awful story. But her imagination filled in some of the blanks.

What had it been like seeing the woman he'd loved living with another man—his own father? Adopting an air of unconcern in public and riding out the storm of speculation that surely must have howled around them all? She cringed thinking of the salacious gossip that must have circulated.

And facing his father—staying loyal and supporting him both publicly and, from what she'd heard, privately too, taking the brunt of responsibility for the kingdom.

She could barely imagine how bereft Raul must have felt at his father's lack of loyalty or caring.

Luisa had been scarred by her grandfather's actions, but at least she'd had the unquestioned support and love of her parents. Raul hadn't had that!

No wonder he closed himself off behind duty and a work schedule that would tax any workaholic. No wonder he found no difficulty marrying without emotion.

Was it possible he could ever learn to trust? To love?

'You're awake.' Dark eyes snared hers and something melted inside.

'You have to go?' Where had that come from? She sounded so needy.

'I'd hoped to stay here.' Heat flickered in his eyes as he took in the shape of her under the sheet. His nostrils flared and suddenly Luisa felt that now-familiar spark of desire flicker into life. Stupid to feel pleased that he obviously didn't relish leaving. It only meant her husband was virile, with an appetite for sex.

A very healthy appetite.

'There was a phone call.' He turned away to pick up his jacket. 'Urgent business.'

It was on the tip of Luisa's tongue to ask what business was so important it interrupted a honeymoon, when she remembered they weren't sharing one. Even the day after the wedding they'd been out and about on public show.

They didn't have that sort of marriage. Theirs was a convenient union. Remember?

She turned away, battling deep sadness.

'I'm sorry, Luisa.' He startled her, speaking from beside the bed. 'This is one matter I can't ignore.' She stared up into his brooding face. 'It's to do with the unrest I mentioned. I'm needed.'

She nodded. He had a country to run. That would always be his priority. Only now did she begin to understand how important that was to him. Through personal crises, his royal responsibilities at least had remained constant. No wonder he was so focused on them. Had they provided solace when he'd most needed it?

'You have a heavy schedule,' she said to fill the silence.

'You get used to it. I've been preparing for the work since I was four.'

The reminder sent a shiver down her spine. Raul had said any child of his would be brought up differently and she'd fight tooth and nail to ensure no child of hers was 'moulded' in that heartless way. She had to make a stand—for herself and for her family if she ever had one.

Luisa sat up against the headboard, drawing the sheet over her breasts and trying to ignore the flash of interest in Raul's eyes.

'I'll get up too. I have plans for this afternoon.'

'Plans? There are no appointments scheduled.'

'I want to meet with Gregor and the other garden-ers. You have no objection to the parterre garden and some of the other spaces being renewed, do you?' It was a spur of the moment decision but she refused to spend the afternoon here, pining over the state of her marriage.

'No, of course not. It's overdue. But I can detail one of my staff to oversee it. It will need consul-tation, not just with the ground staff but with the castle historian, as well as kitchen and event staff. It's not just a matter of gardening.'

'That will be a good way to get to know them.' Luisa needed something to sink her teeth into, something to focus on other than Raul. She didn't want to think about the emotions he inspired for fear of what she'd discover.

'You don't *need* to work, Luisa.'

Her brows rose. 'You expect me to loll in the lap of luxury while you work the day after your wed-ding?'

'I regret that. I'd much prefer to stay.' The glint in his eyes made her pulse hammer erratically but she ignored it.

'I need something to *do*. A purpose. I'd go crazy without that. I'm used to working.'

Raul lifted a hand to his already perfectly knotted

tie and for a split second she'd have said he looked uncomfortable.

'Your lessons don't keep you busy?'

'That's not enough.' She'd never been good at formal lessons. Her language skills were improving but if she had to learn about one more Maritzian monarch or the correct way to greet a grand duke, she'd scream.

Besides, the intensive lessons evoked memories of her long ago stay in Ardissia. The rigid discipline and the judgemental faces were missing, but she couldn't shake the notion she'd never live up to expectations.

Raul surveyed her, his face unreadable. 'Soon you'll be busy with official duties. As my consort there'll be plenty of events where you're required.'

'Being seen at openings and fetes?' She shook her head and sat straighter. 'That's not me.' Despite the makeover, she'd never be the glamorous clothes horse people liked to stare at in magazines. Wearing those stunning couture clothes, she felt like a fraud. Not like herself.

It didn't help, remembering Raul had bought her just as he'd bought them.

'I'll make a start this afternoon.' She met his unblinking gaze, almost challenging him to protest.

When he merely nodded Luisa took a slow breath.

If she was making a new start there was something else she had to face.

'I'm planning to visit Ardissia too.' It was time to lay her grandfather's ghost. Maybe going there, confronting the place that had meant so much to him, and held such dreadful memories for her, would help her bury her hatred.

He frowned. 'My schedule's too full right now.'

Luisa drew herself up. 'Do I need to wait for you? Aren't I Princess of Ardissia?' Much as she disliked the title, it was the one thing she'd got out of this devil's bargain: her inheritance. In her absence the province had become the responsibility of the monarch, but she was here now. 'It's time I shouldered my responsibilities.'

Raul paced towards the bed, his brows arrowing down. 'It's logical we go together. People will expect that.'

'But you're tied up every day. You just said you're not free.' A little breathing space, time to regroup after the massive changes in her life, beckoned. She'd been on a roller coaster of emotion these last weeks.

'There are matters of protocol and plans to be made. Royalty doesn't just stop by.'

Why was he against her going? No mistaking the

tension in his big frame. The tantalising idea surfaced that he'd miss her. She dismissed it instantly.

'It's not dangerous, is it?'

He shook his head. 'Ardissia is safe.'

'Good. I'm sure I'll be welcome. I'll give notice I'm coming. A couple of days. Would that be enough?'

She stared into his set face, suddenly relishing the challenge of standing up to the man who'd taken over her life in more ways than she'd ever bargained for.

She needed to stake a claim as her own person lest he subsume her totally. Even now she longed for him to haul her close and forget the so important appointment that called him away. How was that for needy?

'Surely it's the right thing to do?' She worked to keep a cajoling note from her voice. 'It's only polite to visit now I've accepted my inheritance.'

Raul's lowering brows told her he didn't see it that way. The sight of tension in his jaw sent dangerous excitement zigzagging through her. As if she felt pleasure knowing she got under his skin, even in such a way as this.

Surely she wasn't that desperate for his attention?

'The timing's not ideal, but you're right. A visit makes sense. Leave it with me.'

Why did Luisa feel as if she'd lost the argument when he nodded, turned and strode out of the room, his mind obviously occupied with matters of business?

She hadn't expected him to kiss her, had she?

'This way, Your Highness.' The chamberlain ushered Luisa into her grandfather's study. She'd left it to last on her tour of the Ardissian royal palace.

She pictured the old man here, seated at the massive desk awash with opulent gilt scrollwork. Even in his towering rages he hadn't deigned to rise. Always he'd remembered his position as prince and hers as unsatisfactory, low-born grandchild.

Her teeth clenched as she recalled his poisonous words. Not merely his diatribe on her incompetence and ingratitude but his slashing vitriol at her parents.

'Thank you.' She nodded to the chamberlain, smiling despite his haughty rigidity. 'That's all.'

As he withdrew she considered the portraits lining the walls. Ancestors with remote expressions stared down their noses at her. She lifted her head, surveying the portrait of the man who'd cut off his daughter and his granddaughter when they wouldn't kowtow to his domineering ways.

'The last laugh's on you, Grandad. The farmer's daughter is Princess, soon to be Queen.'

Yet there was no pleasure in the shallow triumph. She hadn't come to gloat, but to see if she could put the past behind her and move on.

She wrapped her arms around herself, suppressing a shiver. Despite her determination to accept her lot, to dress the part and learn protocol and all the other things they foisted on her, Luisa couldn't imagine the future.

What would it hold?

Endless, empty years of public receptions and meaningless small talk? Breathtaking moments of delight when Raul treated her to mind-blowing sex? Heat curled inside at the memory of his loving.

Would she hang onto those moments, desperate for the little Raul could give her when she wanted so much more?

Would her life be sterile of friends and family?

If she had children, how could she protect them from the world that had produced a monster like her grandfather? And Raul had turned into a man of such emotional reserve she wondered if she'd ever build a relationship with him.

She paced to the window, seeking the warmth of the sun streaming in on the luxurious carpet.

Only the best for the Ardissian prince! She'd

seen the rundown sections of the city and the bare amenities provided for the palace servants when she'd insisted on seeing *all* the premises. Her grandfather had spent money on his own comfort rather than his people.

Movement caught her eye. A group of young people made their way across the courtyard. On impulse Luisa opened the window. Laughter, bubbling and fresh, washed around her before they entered a door on the far side of the yard.

Wherever they were going, it appealed more than this place. She closed the window and headed for the door.

Raul drummed his fingers on the car seat as the limo purred towards the Ardissian palace. He lifted a hand to the people lining the street.

He was eager for a break after this intense week. He'd planned to come days ago, but political developments had made it impossible. Now he could please himself.

It pleased him to see his wife.

Five days she'd been away. It seemed far longer. His bed felt empty. His days regimented and predictable, despite the political crisis they'd averted.

Life seemed…less without Luisa.

His lips flattened as he thought of the day she'd

announced she'd come here. He'd only just dragged himself from the temptation of her. He'd reeled from an ecstasy unlike any he'd known. And from the unique sense of peace that came from sharing the story of his past.

Was it simply that he'd needed to unburden himself after years keeping it to himself? He couldn't shake the suspicion that the sensations of release and relief had more to do with the fact it was Luisa he shared with.

Only the most urgent crisis had forced him away, still stunned by the unprecedented sense of peace and pleasure he'd found with her.

And she'd sat there, her sweet mouth a taut line, demanding occupation. *Demanding more.*

Clearly he hadn't been enough to satisfy her!

Male pride smarted from the fact she'd been unaffected by what had passed between them, while it had knocked him completely off balance. It had been on the tip of his tongue to beg her not to leave.

Because he *needed* her! Not just sexually.

He couldn't remember feeling this way about a woman. Even Ana, at the height of her appeal, hadn't invaded his thoughts like this.

Raul smoothed his hand over the seat. At night he found himself reaching for Luisa. He felt bereft when she wasn't there.

Worse was his gut-deep sense of culpability. As the limo pulled up before her ancestral palace, her words came back to haunt him. How desperate she'd been for work to occupy her. Yet another reminder that, despite his attempts to help her adjust, this wasn't the life she'd chosen.

It was the life he'd demanded so he could inherit.

Yes, Maritz needed a strong monarch to see it through difficult times and, with the support of a democratic government, steer it clear of civil war.

But wasn't it also true he'd *needed* to be king? The monarchy had been his salvation as well as his burden as he'd worked to drag himself and his country out of the pit his father's hasty marriage had plunged them into.

And for that he'd bullied Luisa into his world.

He'd wanted to believe she'd find a fulfilling life by his side. These last weeks he'd seen glimpses of a woman who could make the role of consort her own and make a huge difference to his people, even if her way was not the traditional one.

Could she be happy here?

If he'd thought she'd be eager, waiting at the grand staircase to greet him, he was mistaken. Instead it was Lukas, whom he'd sent to support Luisa.

'Your Highness, welcome. And congratulations on the results of your recent negotiations.'

Raul smiled, allowing himself to enjoy anew a sense of relief. 'Thank you, Lukas. Hopefully it will mean peace at last.' He looked around but still no sign of Luisa.

'Her Highness planned to be here. She's delayed but shouldn't be long.' As he spoke he turned, walking with Raul inside the palace.

It was as grand and gloomy as Raul remembered.

He shuddered at the thought of Luisa here, a trusting, innocent teenager, at the mercy of the venomous old man who'd treated her and her mother so appallingly.

'Sorry?'

'I said the chamberlain has requested an audience.'

Raul stopped. 'Surely his business is with my wife. This is her property.'

One look at Lukas' face told Raul there was trouble ahead. He sighed. Days without sleep took their toll. All he wanted was his wife and a bed, in that order.

'Raul!' Luisa slammed to a stop in the doorway to her suite. She'd planned to be back earlier.

Groomed and presentable, ready to greet him with calm courtesy.

One look at him, framed by the arched window, and her breath sawed out of control. Her heart kicked into a frantic rhythm. So much for calm. Just being in the same room with him shattered her composure.

She'd been so busy these last days. It was ridiculous she should miss him, but she had. More than she'd expected.

If things were different, if *they* were different, she'd run over and plant a kiss on his tense mouth until it softened in that sulky, sexy way it did when they were intimate. He'd put his arms around her and…

This was no fantasy. One look at his cool expression scotched that notion.

'Luisa.' He inclined his head but he didn't approach. Something inside her sank. 'How are you?'

'Fine, thanks.' She pushed back the hair that fell over her cheek and surreptitiously straightened her collar. She'd yanked her jacket on in a hurry. 'How was your trip?'

'Excellent.' He paused and she felt tension vibrate between them. 'Though as soon as I arrived your chamberlain came to me.'

Luisa frowned. Now she understood his disapproval. No doubt the official had poured out a litany of complaints. The man had been negative since she'd arrived.

'I see.' She breathed deep. She supposed she'd broken all sorts of rules. Now she had to face the music. But she refused to be intimidated. These were her decisions to make and she'd stick by them.

She closed the door and walked into the room. She gestured to an armchair. Raul ignored it.

'He voiced a number of concerns.'

'I'm sure he did. What did he start with? The proposal to open the state reception rooms for public functions?'

Raul shook his head, his saturnine eyebrows tilting down. 'No. It was your plan to turn the Prince's private apartments into a museum.'

Luisa's chin jerked up. 'I'm never going to use them so they might as well be put to some use.' She swept out a hand that encompassed her bright modern room with its view to the Alps. 'This is more suitable for when I visit.' She shuddered. 'All that overdecorated pomposity downstairs is too much for me.' Besides, the thought of bunking in her grandsire's bed curdled her blood.

'For us.' Raul paced closer.

'Sorry?'

'We'll visit together in future.'

What? He didn't trust her now to come here without him? She drew herself up to her full height.

'What else did he object to?' Might as well get it over, though it stuck in her craw to defend her plans.

Raul spread his arms in a gesture that drew her eyes to the expanse of his chest. She remembered his strength as he'd pulled her into his arms and taken her to heaven.

Despite her anger, heat snaked through her belly.

'He had a list. He was concerned about the plans for a children's playgroup in the eastern annexe.'

Luisa's mouth tightened. 'The premises are perfect and easily accessible from the main square. You might not know but in this part of the city there's virtually no provision for community groups. It's not like central Maritz where that's well catered for.'

It seemed her grandfather had stymied local plans to support the community, especially young people. His mindset had been rooted in the past.

'And the cooking school?'

She put her hands on her hips. 'I found students visiting the old kitchens. Their premises had been damaged when the old wiring caused a fire. The palace chef offered temporary use of the kitchens here.' Her lips firmed. 'It's a perfect match. The facilities are here, and the expertise for that matter. It's not as if there are lots of state banquets since I'm not here permanently.'

'And the same for the mechanics?'

She stared. 'How do you know about that?' She'd just come from a meeting of vocational teachers in what had been the stables but now housed an automotive workshop.

Raul stepped towards her and she read a flicker of something in his eyes that made the heat in her belly spread low and deep.

He raised a hand to her cheek. Luisa shuddered as delicious sensation stirred. She didn't want this distraction, this sweet reminder of the magic he wrought!

'It was a guess.' He held up his hand so she saw a dark stain. 'Motor oil?'

Her tongue thickened at his nearness. He was so close his body heat invaded her space.

'We were checking the facilities and I got a little…involved.'

Raul's eyes narrowed. 'I see. Like you got *involved* when you were presented with that cow?'

Luisa clenched her hands rather than spread them in a pleading gesture. The press had had a field day with that and she'd avoided reading the paper for days since. One paper in particular delighted in portraying her as wilful and disrespectful, though most seemed positive.

The animal had been beautiful, with garlands of flowers round its neck and horns and a huge alpine bell.

'It was part of the official welcome to Ardissia. Lukas explained it was a sign of great respect from the rural population. I couldn't refuse it!'

'But did you have to milk it?' His mouth tightened till the strain showed at his jaw.

She shrugged, feeling hemmed in by his disapproval. 'OK, so it wasn't proper protocol. I know real princesses wouldn't dream of it. But we got talking about dairy cattle and suddenly they offered me a milking stool and a bucket and...' She threw up her hands. 'So sue me! You insisted I do this. Don't complain now that I'm unorthodox. I'm trying. And—' she jabbed a finger into his pristine shirt '—while I'm happy to hear suggestions about these ideas for the palace, it's ultimately *my* decision. No one else's!'

'Exactly what I told your chamberlain.'

'Sorry?' Luisa was so dazed she barely noticed Raul had closed his hand around her prodding finger.

'I told him to keep his thoughts to himself until he had a chance to share them with you.'

Luisa stared. 'You don't mind?'

His nostrils flared. 'I mind very much being accosted by a jumped-up official who bad-mouths his employer behind her back. And I'm furious.'

Her shoulders sank. Here it came.

'Furious I didn't have the right to fire the troublemaker on the spot. He's your employee but he's more concerned about his own prestige than his job!'

'Raul?' Only now did she notice his other arm had slipped round to drag her close. She inhaled his intoxicating scent. It was like reliving those intense dreams that had haunted her ever since she'd come here.

'It's your decision, Luisa. But you need to consider finding someone better. Someone who can work with you on your plans rather than thwart them.'

She locked her knees against the trembling that started somewhere near her heart and spread to her limbs.

'You don't *mind* what I've been doing?' She'd been so sure of his disapproval her brain struggled with any other explanation for his tight-lipped expression.

'Why should I mind?' He rubbed her back in a circling motion that eased muscles drawn to breaking point. 'It's good to see you getting involved and listening to your people. I'm proud of what you've tackled in such a short space of time. But you're sensible enough to take advice and not rush into anything without due consideration.'

She blinked, staring up into dark green eyes that glimmered with warmth. The shock of it nearly undid her.

After the chamberlain's starchy disapproval and the knowledge her grandfather would roll in his grave at her plans for his precious palace, she hadn't been surprised to read criticism in Raul's expression.

Except now she couldn't find it.

A wave of warmth crashed over her that had nothing to do with Raul's nearness. It stemmed from an inner glow, knowing he'd stood up for her with the chamberlain.

That he was ready to support her.

That he seemed to care.

She put out another trembling hand to his chest, spreading her fingers to capture the steady beat of his heart. His arm tightened around her and he leaned close.

'But what I most want to know, wife, is what the mayor said when you presented him with a bucket of warm milk.'

Again she caught that flicker in his eyes, the tightening of his lips. This time she realised what it was.

Raul trying not to laugh.

'He was very impressed and told me I had hidden talents.' Her mouth twitched. 'Then he showed me an old local technique he reckons gives you a better grip.'

Raul's face creased into a smile, then a grin. He tipped his head back and released a deep infectious laugh that made her lips curve and her heart dance.

Deep within Luisa something relaxed, unfurled and spread.

Happiness.

CHAPTER TWELVE

THAT happiness stayed. It was like a glowing ember, warming her from the inside and thawing the chill that had gripped her so long.

With each week Luisa found herself more content. She grew fond of her new home and its people. The nation of Maritz and even its tiny principality of Ardissia that she'd recalled as a nightmare place from her youth were growing more like home. She could be happy here.

Then there was Raul. He could be gentle and tender but there was always an undercurrent of explosive passion between them that left her breathless. Luisa shivered as erotic memories surfaced. Their physical intimacy was out of this world, and she always felt she got close then to the real man behind the façade.

The man she wanted to know better.

Raul was a loner. No wonder, with such a regimented childhood, brought up by staff rather than doting parents. Then there was his father's betrayal with the woman Raul had fallen for.

He'd spent so long cutting himself off from emotional connections; the moments when he let down his guard with her were special, poignantly precious.

More and more, Raul shared his wry wit, surprising her into giggles of shock or delight. The last thing she'd expected from the man who'd married her to claim the crown.

But as she watched him work tirelessly for his country, every day and into the night, and saw his people respond to him, she knew he was the right man for the job.

Luisa's anger over his ruthless actions was now strangely muted. She knew Raul wasn't the unfeeling villain she'd once painted him. In some ways he was as much a victim of circumstance as she. A wounded man who hid his vulnerability behind a façade.

She felt melancholy. For, despite the way he stood up for her, supporting her sometimes unorthodox approach to her royal duties, she could never forget that for him she was an unwanted wife.

The wife he had to have.

A sweet ache pierced her and she pressed a hand to her chest. She hitched a breath and stared blindly at the newspaper on the desk before her.

It hurt because, even knowing Raul made the best of their convenient marriage, Luisa had done the unthinkable.

She'd fallen in love.

Despite the pain, happiness bubbled. Ripples of delight shivered through her till she trembled.

Love was such a big emotion. It overcame the fears plaguing her.

Surely there was a way she could make this marriage work? Make him care for her the way she cared for him?

'Sitting alone, Luisa?' Raul's voice made her jump and turn. Her heart kicked as she took in his tall frame, his sculpted features and the flare of heat in his eyes.

She yearned to throw herself into his embrace. Declare her feelings and demand he love her too.

If only it were that simple.

She sat where she was, limbs stiffening as she strove not to give herself away. He'd be horrified if he guessed her feelings. She had to be calm while inside she was a nervous jumble of joy and fear and tentative hope.

'My language lesson's over and I was trying to read the paper.' She twisted her fingers together and looked down, choosing an article at random.

'There's a picture of you but the words are too difficult.'

He stood behind her. She knew from the way her flesh prickled. Her body possessed radar tuned solely to Raul. Whenever he approached, even when he watched her from the other side of a crowded reception, Luisa felt it.

'It's a court report. Why not try something simpler?' His words were a puff of warmth at her ear as he leaned in.

Luisa shut her eyes, willing him to forget the paper and slide his arms around her.

'Luisa?'

She snapped her eyes open. 'What's the article about?' She didn't care but she had to say something.

'Just the trial of people illegally stockpiling banned weapons. Why don't we—'

'But why were you a witness?' She'd finally made sense of the caption.

'It's not that exciting.'

She frowned, finally concentrating on the piece. 'It says something about an armed raid. And a plot. A coup.' That word was familiar. She pointed at the next paragraph. 'What's that word?'

A sigh riffled her hair. He hesitated so long she wondered if he'd answer. 'Assassination.'

Luisa swung round, shock widening her eyes.

'Who did they want to assassinate?' Ice froze her feet, her legs, creeping upwards as she read resignation in Raul's expression.

Surely it couldn't have been…

'The cabinet. As many government officials as they could.' He straightened and stepped away and she felt bereft. She pushed back her chair and stood on shaky legs.

'And the Prince?' The words were a brittle rasp from her constricting throat. 'They wanted to kill you?'

To her horror he didn't deny it, merely lifted his shoulders. 'Don't worry, Luisa, it was over weeks ago, when you went to Ardissia.'

The glacial frost encroached to her heart and she wrapped her arms around herself. 'You didn't tell me.'

He strode to her and rubbed his hands over her rigid arms. 'You have nothing to fear, honestly. It's all over.'

'You think I'm worried for myself?'

Raul's eyes widened and for an instant she saw a flicker of shock. Then he drew her close. Beneath her ear she heard the strong beat of his heart. Her hands slid under his jacket, palming the muscled heat of his torso.

He was so alive. So vibrant. If anything happened to him…

Terror was a jagged blade, slicing through her.

This was the downside of love. She cared so much for Raul the thought of losing him was impossible to bear.

He moved to step back but she burrowed closer. His arms tightened till she felt cocooned and safe.

'Listen, Luisa. It really is over. These were just a handful of the lunatic fringe. The police had monitored them for some time so there was no danger. In fact their schemes have done everyone a favour.'

'How?' She arched back to meet his eyes.

'I told you there'd been unrest. It got worse in the final stages of my father's reign.' Raul paused before finally continuing.

'There were limits to what I could achieve as prince. In the last years as his marriage deteriorated, he became…erratic. He let his cronies grab too much power and didn't think strategically about the nation's well-being. Power blocs have been vying for position.'

'Lukas said you'd worked to keep the peace.'

'Did he? It looked at one stage as if the various parties might tear the country apart. The news that unstable elements saw that as an opportunity for a bloodbath made them all rethink and realise how important our peace and democracy are. It's brought them back to the negotiating table.' He smoothed his hand over her hair in a gentle caress.

'When the coronation takes place and parliament resumes, we'll be working together.'

'But what about—'

A finger against her lips stopped her words. 'It's nothing to concern you.' He turned to the newspaper. 'Let me find you something easier to read.'

Luisa's mind whirled. Raul had been in danger for his life. She'd assumed his talk of protecting the country was exaggerated to cover his desire to inherit.

Her stomach hollowed, realising how serious the situation had been. That she might have lost him.

That he hadn't considered sharing even a little of the truth with her. Even now he didn't want her to know.

And she'd thought they'd been building a rapport!

Raul might support her attempts to become a princess. He might take her to paradise with his body. But as for sharing anything more significant… How could she pretend it was possible when he kept so much from her?

Pain twisted to raw anguish in Luisa's heart. Even if he didn't carry a torch for Ana, his distrust was so ingrained Luisa saw now her chances of truly connecting with him were doomed.

He was a man she could love. The man she *did* love—strong, caring, capable and tender. But she knew no way to breach the final brittle shell of reserve he wore like armour. The shell that kept them apart even when she'd imagined they shared more and more.

She'd fooled herself, believing that after their time together he'd begun to feel something for her too.

He wouldn't want to hear her declaration of love.

He didn't want to share himself.

How would he react if she told him she suspected he'd shared enough of himself to create a child with her?

CHAPTER THIRTEEN

'THIS way, Your Highness.'

Raul followed the urban planner across waste ground, listening to him extol the virtues of the site that would become a community garden. Another of Luisa's projects.

It had merely taken mention of unused public land in a disadvantaged area for Luisa to find a use for it. Castle staff lent expertise to help the community build a place to meet, play and grow food. But it was Luisa, with Lukas' help, who'd checked zoning restrictions, negotiated with the council and met with residents.

His wife had extraordinary organisational skills, honed keeping a struggling business afloat. He'd seen with pleasure how she put those skills to use in Ardissia and here in the capital.

Raul admired her practicality, her drive to make things better.

Who'd have thought a girl off the farm would be such a success? She was a breath of fresh air, cutting through hidebound protocol with a smile, yet sensitive enough to see when tradition was necessary.

People loved her, drawn by her charm and warmth, and the royal fairy tale romance was a source of real pleasure after difficult political times.

Raul urged the planner towards the group at the centre of the site. Luisa was there, wearing her trademark casual chic clothes. He stifled a smile, seeing a couple of girls in almost matching gear.

Luisa's couture gowns were seen now only at formal functions. Instead she'd set her own trend, the first Maritzian royal to wear casual clothes to meet the people. But on Luisa casual looked so good. Today she wore slim-fitting jeans, low-heeled boots of supple scarlet and a matching jacket over a white top.

Only this time she hadn't shoved up her sleeves so she could take a hands-on role. Her boots were pristine, not even a fleck of dirt. Her face wasn't flushed with exertion and she didn't have a hair out of place as when she'd cuddled some toddler in a crowd.

He liked it when she looked a little flushed and rumpled. It reminded him of Luisa naked in his bed.

Now she looked elegant with her stylish clothes and pale, fine-boned features.

Raul's eyes narrowed. Too pale, surely?

Usually Luisa was a golden girl with her colouring and her tan. It complemented her infectious smile as she chatted with anybody and everybody.

Now, though surrounded by people as usual, she stood a little aloof, hanging back from the discussion. She looked peaky and the smile she wore wasn't the grin he'd become accustomed to.

No one else seemed to sense anything wrong.

But he'd come to know his wife.

He tensed, premonition skating down his nape as he recalled recent changes he'd preferred not to dwell on. Times when Luisa's warm impulsiveness had grown strained, appearing only in the heights of passion.

Then she was all his, just as he wanted her.

He repressed a scowl. Did he imagine she'd grown cooler? The suspicion had hit several times that she no longer wanted to share herself. As if she tried to hide the woman he'd come to think of as the real Luisa. Open, honest and exuberant.

Or as if that Luisa had ceased to exist.

An icy hand gripped his innards as he fought a rising tide of tension. A sense of déjà vu.

He squashed the thought. Luisa was *not* Ana.

Only Raul's youth and the blindness of so-called love had ever convinced him Ana was the sort of woman he could trust.

Yet still he couldn't shift a sense of foreboding.

'Is everything OK?'

Luisa swung round, away from people waving goodbye. Raul had moved across the limo's wide seat to settle beside her. He'd raised the privacy screen.

Excitement zinged through her veins and drew the skin of her breasts and stomach tight. Her body betrayed her. She couldn't resist Raul, even knowing their relationship was tragically one-sided. Lately too, the more she tried to pull back and develop some protective distance, the more determined he seemed to invade her space.

Yet there was no gleam in his eyes now, just the shadow of a frown.

'Of course. Everything's fine.' With a supreme effort Luisa pasted a smile on her lips as she lied.

She teetered on a knife-edge of despair. She'd given her heart to a man who couldn't reciprocate her feelings. And now it seemed possible there'd be a child.

Her emotions were like a seesaw. One moment she was thrilled at the idea of carrying Raul's baby, at the new life she hoped she cradled in her womb. The next chill fear gripped her at the idea of bringing a child into this tiny family so unlike anything she'd dreamed of. Love was anathema to Raul yet it was her hidden secret. What sort of world was that in which to raise a child?

That was when she hoped against hope the pregnancy was a false alarm and guilt ate her, for wishing away such a precious gift.

She couldn't blame Raul. With his past it was no wonder he'd cut himself off from the deepest of emotions. She didn't even know if he believed in love!

As for his unswerving dedication to his country, putting it ahead of personal relationships, she could understand that too.

When she'd translated the papers about that trial she'd been stunned to learn the key role Raul had played in the investigation, as well as the political ramifications of the plot. Maritz needed Raul even more than Raul needed the satisfaction of fulfilling the role he was born to.

'Luisa?'

'Yes?' She looked over his shoulder and waved. 'What did you think of the garden site? It's got potential, don't you think? And the locals are very enthusiastic.' Great. Now she was babbling.

'The site is excellent.' He paused and she sensed he chose his words carefully. 'You seem…not as exuberant as usual.'

Luisa darted a glance at him then away, her stomach churning. 'I didn't think exuberance in a princess was a good thing.' She clenched nervous hands and searched for a neutral topic. 'The project's going well, don't you think?' Or had she already said that? Her brain was scrambled.

'Very well. You should be pleased.'

'I am. The volunteers have worked so hard.'

'You've worked hard too.' His brows puckered. 'You haven't been overdoing it, have you?'

Luisa's breath snagged. Had he guessed? She'd been forced from bed earlier and earlier by what she suspected was morning sickness. She didn't want Raul to see her white, nauseous and bedraggled. Especially when she didn't know how he'd react to the news.

It was one thing for him to say he'd break with tradition in bringing up a child. Another to welcome their baby with the whole-hearted love it deserved.

In that moment she decided. The idea of a trip home to see Mary and Sam had lurked in the back of her mind for days. Now the need for their warmth and unquestioning support was too much to resist. She'd visit them and discreetly schedule a doctor's appointment, something that was impossible here. Imagine even visiting a pharmacy in Maritz to buy a pregnancy test kit! The news would be in the press before nightfall.

Luisa needed time and space to come to grips with the changes in her life. She'd go as soon as the coronation was over.

'Of course I haven't overdone it. I'm fit as ever.'

He placed his hands over hers. Instantly she froze. She hadn't realised she'd been wringing them. His warmth flowed into her and for a moment her racing brain calmed. Perhaps after all she could—

'You didn't cross the site to say hello to the people on the far side of the block.'

Luisa drew a steadying breath. 'We'd run out of time. I know you have a meeting and I'd already been there a while before you arrived.'

'Still—' his gaze pierced hers '—normally you make time for everyone.'

'You wanted to see them?' She'd been so eager to get away, to find quiet in which to think.

'No, you're right.' He shook his head. 'I'd run out of time. It just seemed…unlike you.'

Luisa flexed her fingers and instantly he released his grip and moved away.

Pain gripped her chest.

See? It wasn't that he wanted to hold her. Except of course when they had sex. He was just making sure she was well enough to carry out her duties.

Raul's meeting had been endless. Time and again he'd caught himself staring at his watch, calculating how long before he could get away.

He should be pleased. All was set for the coronation next week and negotiations with formerly difficult local leaders had proved fruitful.

Yet he couldn't concentrate. Luisa had seemed strained earlier this afternoon. This morning he'd woken to find she'd slipped from his bed again. What had begun as an occasional irritation was now a worrying habit.

He felt unsettled when she wasn't there. He liked waking with her. Not only for the physical satisfaction of early morning sex. But because she made him feel good. Relaxed. Content.

Strange, when in the past he'd preferred to sleep alone. But so many things about his marriage were unusual.

Like the way he watched Luisa. She was vibrant and attractive, though not as gorgeous as some women he'd known. Yet he found himself watching her all the time, smiling when she smiled, enjoying her interactions with others and her combination of spunk and intelligence during their own discussions.

Though there hadn't been many of those lately. His fingers tightened on the neck of the chilled champagne bottle. Tonight would be different.

He put his head in the outer office before leaving for the private apartments.

'Clear my calendar for the fortnight after the coronation, can you?' He was determined to spend time alone with Luisa. Now things were stable he'd take time off and give her a honeymoon they'd both enjoy.

He couldn't think of anything he enjoyed more than being with his wife.

'Yes, sir.' The junior secretary took a note.

'Don't book anything else in my wife's diary either. I'll talk to her about clearing her dates as well.'

He smiled. A couple of weeks at his secluded lakeside retreat. It would be beautiful at this time of year. Luisa would love it and they could be alone.

'I'm sorry, sir.' The girl frowned. 'The princess is booked on a flight the day after the coronation.'

'A flight? It must be a mistake.'

'No, sir. I organised it myself just hours ago.'

Raul felt a curious hollow sensation deep in his chest. He strode to the computer.

'Show me.'

Silently she found the booking then turned the screen towards him. A flight to Sydney, no stop-overs. No return.

The void in Raul's chest expanded and the breath seared from his lungs.

'Was there a call from Australia?' It might be sickness in the family. Luisa was close to her aunt and uncle.

But she hadn't mentioned it to him.

'Not that I know of, Your Highness.'

She bit her lip and Raul realised he was looming over her, glowering. He took a step back and forced a smile.

'That's fine. I'll talk to her about it myself.' He turned on his heel. A sixth sense chilled his flesh.

A one-way ticket to Sydney. Alone.

He forced down the instant thought that she'd had enough. That Luisa couldn't stand it here, had never forgiven him for bringing her to Maritz and planned to leave for good. *Leave him.*

His skin prickled and he lengthened his stride.

There would be an explanation. Yet his belly was a hard twist of tension as he headed for the royal apartments.

Raul tapped on the door of her suite and waited.

Strange. According to the secretary, Luisa had come here an hour ago to rest.

He knocked again and turned the handle. Perhaps she'd fallen asleep on the bed. Despite his concern, Raul's mouth kicked up at the idea of Luisa, tousled and soft from sleep.

He stepped in and slammed to a stop.

Time splintered.

He stood frozen, bile rising as his numb mind absorbed details. Déjà vu smote him and he reeled.

Yet this was worse. Far worse. This was Luisa…

Luisa and Lukas.

This clearly was no business meeting but something far more intimate.

Luisa wore a tight tank top and flirty skirt, her hands curled round Lukas' shoulders. Lukas, the man he would have trusted with his life! *The man he'd trusted with Luisa.*

Lukas held her close in his embrace, arms wrapped possessively round her slim form. Their blond heads were just a kiss apart.

Raul recalled his wife's recent coolness, the way she left his bed and tried to distance herself. Had Raul been a coward, ignoring signs he didn't want to see? Could Luisa have betrayed him as Ana had?

It felt as if someone had reached in and ripped his heart out.

Lukas had removed his jacket and tie. His collar was undone. Had Luisa done that? Had she used her nimble fingers to begin undressing him?

Roaring pain blasted Raul. It battered like a mountain avalanche till he could barely stand upright. It clamped his chest in a vice so tight he couldn't draw breath.

An explosion of shattering glass at his feet roused him from sick shock. The couple before him whipped their heads round and noticed him.

Fiery colour washed Luisa's face and her hands dropped. Lukas straightened and released her, adjusting his collar.

Raul's brain filled with an image he couldn't thrust away. Of Ana and his father, emerging from a state bedroom after his old man had taken Raul's visitor on a personal tour. Ana had coloured and looked away. His father had stood straighter, fiddling with his cuffs.

The beginning of their betrayal.

Raul breathed deep. With an effort he cleared his whirling thoughts.

This was Luisa and Lukas. Not Ana and his father.

His heart thundered and adrenalin pumped in his blood, but sanity prevailed. He forced his stiff legs to move. Ignoring the churning in his belly, he prowled into the room.

Raul watched Luisa's bright flush fade and her skin pale to bone-white.

'Luisa.' His voice sounded unfamiliar.

'Your Highness.' Lukas hurried into speech. 'I know this must look—'

Raul slashed one silencing hand through the air. It was Luisa he needed to talk with.

'But Your Highness…Raul…'

Raul swung round, focusing on his secretary. Through all the years they'd worked together Lukas had been a stickler for formality, refusing Raul's suggestion more than once that in private Lukas call him by name.

Fear churned in Raul's belly that Lukas should choose this moment to bridge that gap. To put them on equal footing.

Why? Because he and Luisa…?

No! Raul refused to let himself think it.

Yet, like a spectre, the possibility hovered in the recesses of his brain, waiting to swamp him in a moment of weakness.

'Leave us, Lukas.'

His voice was harsh with shock and a fear greater than anything he'd known.

Still Lukas didn't move, but looked to Luisa who stood, fingers threading nervously before her.

'Go, Lukas,' she whispered. 'It will be all right.'

Finally, with lagging steps he left. Raul heard the door click quietly behind him. Yet still Luisa didn't meet his eyes.

Anxiety stretched each nerve to breaking point. He clenched his hands, forcing himself to wait till she was ready to talk.

'It's not what you think.'

'You don't know what I'm thinking.' At this moment rational thought was almost beyond him. He was a mass of churning emotions. Only the voice that told him over and over that Luisa was *different*, was *his*, kept him sane.

She lifted her head and met his gaze and the familiar sizzle in his veins eased a fraction of the desperate tension in his body.

This was his Luisa. He refused to believe the worst.

'Aren't you going to ask about Lukas?'

'I know you'll tell me.' He just prayed he was man enough to hear the truth.

She paced away, her steps short, her eyes averted as if she couldn't bear to look at him. Fear knotted his brain.

'He was helping me.'

'Go on.'

'He was teaching me to dance.'

'Sorry?' Raul stared, flummoxed by the unexpected response.

'Teaching me to waltz, ready for the coronation ball.' Luisa flashed him a challenging look. 'At home our local dance was a disco in the school hall and I never learnt anything formal.' She looked at a point over his shoulder. 'It didn't matter at our wedding because the country was in mourning and there was no dancing at the reception, but this time…' She shrugged stiffly. 'I didn't want to disgrace you on your big day.'

Raul frowned. There was something so intimate about the idea of teaching Luisa to waltz. Holding her in his arms and showing her how to move her body with his.

'You could have asked me.' Surely that was the sort of thing husbands did? He'd have revelled in it.

What did it say about their marriage that she'd turned to his *secretary* to help her?

Colour washed her throat and her mouth pursed. 'And make it obvious there was another simple thing I couldn't do? You have no idea how hard it's been to try to get everything right—the protocol and customs and language—and still I make so many mistakes. Besides—' she drew a shaky breath '—it's so basic. How embarrassing not even to know how to waltz.'

She blinked quickly and his heart compressed.

'I don't care if you can't dance.' His voice was rough as he stepped closer.

'But I do. I wanted…' She chewed her lip.

'You thought anyone would care about your dancing ability? That I'd care? That's absurd!' Not after they'd shared so much. More than he'd shared with any other woman.

'Absurd?' She shook her head and spun away to pace the room again.

Raul wanted to tug her into his arms but the way she wrapped her arms round her torso and her strained expression told him this wasn't the time.

'What's really absurd is marrying someone you don't know. Giving yourself to someone who'll never care for you. Can never care for you because he never got over the woman who hurt him years ago.'

Shock held Raul mute as her words lashed him. He couldn't credit what he heard. Luisa believed he hadn't got over Ana?

'That's not true!'

He reached for her, took her arm, but she shrugged out of his grasp.

Anguish lacerated him at her rejection.

'Do you know how it feels knowing I wasn't your first choice of wife, not even your second? That you married me because of who my grandfather was?'

She drew a huge shuddering sigh and Raul felt the full weight of regret bear down on him for all he'd done to this vibrant, special woman.

All through their relationship his needs had come first. She'd given him what he wanted, more than he'd ever dreamed possible, and all the time she'd suffered.

He'd known it, had felt pangs of guilt but never before had he truly faced the full magnitude of Luisa's distress and loss. He'd conned himself into believing she'd begun to feel some of the pleasure he did in their union, shared some of his hopes for the future.

Reality hit him like a sledgehammer to the heart.

Raul shoved trembling hands into his pockets rather than reach for her. Clearly she didn't want his touch. The knowledge burned like acid.

'Is that why you've booked a flight to Sydney next week?'

Luisa's mouth gaped then shut with a snap. 'You know about that?'

'I just found out.' He waited. When she remained silent he prompted, hoping against hope there was another reason for her trip. 'Is there a family emergency?'

She shook her head and he felt hope flicker and fade.

'I wanted to go home.' Her voice cracked and it was all Raul could do not to scoop her close.

'This is your home.' His voice was rough, emotion scouring each word.

She shook her head so fervently fine gold hair whirled around her face and he'd have sworn her eyes shimmered with tears. His stomach clenched as from a crippling blow.

'I need time. Time away from here.'

Time away from him.

Something withered in Raul's breast. Something he couldn't put a name to. He'd hoped eventually she'd be happy with him, forget how he'd forced her to come here. Had he deluded himself, believing she'd come to care for him? That they'd begun to share something special?

But he couldn't give up.

'You belong here now, Luisa.'

He cut himself off before he could say she belonged to *him*.

'Do I?' She spun away, her arms wrapped over her chest. She drew a shuddering breath. 'I think it would be wise if I went away for a while. You see—'

'Running away, Luisa?' He couldn't be hearing this. Only yesterday she'd snuggled, naked in his embrace, and he'd felt…he'd hoped…

She shook her head. 'You'll be crowned. You'll have what you want.' Her voice sounded muffled.

And what if it was *her* he wanted? It struck him with the force of absolute truth that he wanted nothing more than to spend his life with Luisa.

Why had he not seen it so clearly before?

The crown, even his country, meant nothing without Luisa.

Had he lost her for good?

Unbidden, an image rose of her and Lukas. Would they meet in Australia?

He refused to consider the possibility.

'You can't leave the day after the coronation. At least put off the trip for a while.' He needed time to make her see reason. Time to convince her to stay.

She stiffened. 'I thought I should be there for the ceremony. But maybe it would be better if—'

She stopped as his mobile phone beeped insistently. With an impatient click of his tongue Raul reached into his pocket and switched it off.

'That's your private line. It's probably important.'

He stalked towards her, in no mood to be distracted. '*This* is important, Luisa.'

The sound of Luisa's landline ringing cut across his words. Before he could prevent her, she'd lifted the receiver, as if eager for the interruption.

'It's for you.' She held out the receiver to him. 'The government's legal counsel says he has to speak with you.'

Raul hesitated. They needed to discuss this now. But the matter he'd had the lawyers working on would surely help his cause with Luisa. He was desperate enough to clutch at anything that would help.

He reached for the phone.

Luisa watched Raul, so intent on the lawyer's news.

See? She'd been right about his priorities. As his wife she came somewhere near the bottom.

He'd challenged her about her trip to Australia and she'd waited, half dreading, half hoping he'd decree she couldn't go, say she had to remain, not for reasons of state but because he couldn't bear to be parted from her.

She'd imagined being swept into his arms, hauled against his hard torso and imprisoned there. Because he loved her as she loved him and he refused to release her.

Reality was so different.

'There's something I need to attend to.'

Wearily she nodded. There'd always be something more important than the state of their marriage. Dejectedly she wondered if perhaps it would be better if she left and didn't return.

'Luisa, did you hear me?'

'Sorry?' She looked up to find him already reaching for the door.

'I said we need to talk, *properly*. I'll be back as soon as I can.'

Luisa nodded, donning the mask of composure that now felt brittle enough to crack. Or was that her heart? Her last hope for a real marriage had just shattered.

CHAPTER FOURTEEN

'THANK YOU, everyone.' Raul nodded to the High Court judges, the Attorney General and the other witnesses who'd been urgently summoned two hours ago on his orders to witness this history-altering event.

In other circumstances he'd be excited at the prospect of initiating such significant change. But it was all he could do to wait patiently while they filed slowly from the chamber, leaving him alone.

So alone.

His mind snagged on the image of Luisa just hours ago in her room, pale and strained as she spoke of the need to get away. The hurt she'd felt at her place in his life.

How deeply he'd injured her, forcing her into his world.

Was he doing the right thing now, trying to tie her to him more strongly than ever? He looked at the parchment on the desk, checked, signed, countersigned and witnessed. The document he'd long planned as a surprise for Luisa, a testament of his regard for her.

The document that now represented his last-ditch, desperate effort to convince her to stay.

Did he have the right to try to hold her when life with him had made her so patently unhappy?

Until today he'd thought her content. More than content: happy.

Was he doomed never to find that emotional closeness Luisa had spoken of so longingly? Was he simply not the right man to make her happy?

Pain seared through his clenched jaw at the notion of letting her go.

Terror engulfed him at the thought of life without her.

But who could blame her? He'd never experienced real love and surely that lack had left him emotionally flawed. Was he incapable of providing what she needed in a husband?

If she wanted to be here it would be different. Together they could face anything. If she cared for him…

His bark of raw laughter was loud in the silence. How could Luisa care for him after what he'd done to her? He'd deluded himself, believing things had changed between them these past weeks. The way she'd shied from his touch this evening said it all.

He turned to the window and looked at the glitter of city lights below. Normally he enjoyed the view of the capital he loved, the valley that had been home to his family for centuries. That sense of place, of belonging, always brought comfort.

Not now. Now all he felt was the terrible aloneness.

Life without Luisa.

He couldn't conceive it. His brain shut down every time he thought about it and a terrible hollow ache filled him. His very hands shook at the idea of her on a plane to Australia without him.

He should do the honourable thing and let her go. Release her from this life she'd never desired.

Yet he wanted to throw back his head and howl his despair at the idea of losing her. His pulse raced and his skin prickled with sweat at the thought of never seeing her again. Never holding her.

Never telling her how he felt.

Excruciating pain ripped at him, giant talons that tore at his soul.

It was no good, try as he might to be self-sacrificing, this was more than he could bear. It was asking too much.

He grabbed the parchment and rolled it quickly, heedless of the still drying wax seals. Turning on his heel he strode to the door.

* * *

Luisa woke slowly, clinging to a surprisingly wonderful dream.

After hours pacing the floor she'd retreated to bed. And still she'd tortured herself reliving the blank look on Raul's face as he'd left her, already intent on other business. The fact that he hadn't countermanded her trip to Sydney. That he didn't care.

Now she felt…safe, cocooned in a warm haven that protected her from everything. She didn't want to move.

But she had no choice. Even in her half aware state she registered the sick feeling, the rising nausea. She breathed deep, trying to force it back but it was no good.

With a desperate lurch she struggled upright, only to find her movements impeded by the large man wrapped around her back. His legs spooned hers, his palm on her stomach.

'Raul!' It was a raw croak. What was he doing here? When had he—?

Her stomach heaved and she thrust his confining arm away, swinging her legs off the bed.

'Luisa!' His voice was sharp. 'What's wrong?'

She had no time for explanations. She stumbled across the room, one hand to her stomach, the other clamped to her mouth as she tasted bile.

Miraculously the bathroom door swung open and she dived in just in time to brace herself as her last meal resurfaced. Her legs wobbled so much her knees folded and she almost crumpled to the floor.

But an arm lashed round her, keeping her upright with all Raul's formidable strength. Behind her she felt his body, hot and solid, anchoring her.

Then she bent, retching as the paroxysm of nausea overcame her. Her skin prickled horribly and searing bitterness filled her as her stomach spasmed again and again till there was nothing more to bring up.

She slumped, trembling and spent, eyes closed as she tried to summon strength to move.

Her head spun, or did she imagine movement? Next thing she knew she was seated on the side of the bath and she sighed her gratitude as every muscle melted. Raul supported her and she couldn't summon the energy to order him out. Not when he was all that kept her upright.

Then, like a blessing, a damp cloth brushed her forehead, her cheeks and throat, her dry lips. She turned her face into it gratefully.

'Drink this.' A glass nudged her mouth. Gratefully she sipped cool water. The damp cloth wiped her forehead again and she almost moaned in relief. She was weak as a kitten.

How could she face Raul now? Why was he here?

Tears stung as exhaustion and self-pity flooded her.

'You're ill. I'll call a doctor.' She opened her eyes to meet a worried dark green gaze. Raul looked grim.

She wanted to sit, basking in her husband's concern, pretending it meant more than it surely did.

'No. I'm not ill. It's perfectly normal. A doctor won't help with this.'

Belatedly she realised what she'd said as Raul's brows arched. Shock froze his features as he read the implications of her nausea.

She'd meant to tell him soon. But not like this.

'Please,' she said quickly. 'I need privacy to freshen up.' She refused to have this conversation on the edge of the bath, with her hair matted across her clammy brow.

Luisa turned away, not wanting to see suspicion darken his gaze. Pain welled and she bit her lip. After seeing her with Lukas it would be no surprise if Raul questioned the baby's paternity. He hadn't said he believed her explanation of why she'd been in Lukas' embrace.

Raul left the room without a word.

She should have been grateful but felt only

despair that he'd been eager to go. So much for her fantasy of them bonding over their child!

Luisa took her time in the bathroom, but when she opened the door Raul was there. To her astonishment he swooped, scooping her into his arms.

'I can walk.' But her protest was half-hearted. His embrace was magic, even knowing it didn't mean anything. Raul was a man for whom duty was paramount. Tending to a pregnant female would come naturally.

He deposited her on the bed, where plumped up pillows sat against the headboard. He drew the coverlet over her and reached for something on the bedside table.

'Here. Try this.' It was a plate of salted crackers. He must have ordered them while she was in the bathroom.

'I'm not an invalid.' Luisa pushed them aside and fought not to succumb to the sweet delight of being cared for. Absurdly, the thoughtful gesture made her eyes swim, despite her anger and distress.

It didn't help that Raul looked wonderful. Faded denim stretched across his taut, powerful thighs. He wore a black pullover, sleeves bunched up to reveal strong, sinewy forearms. He was even more gorgeous than in one of his suave suits. Would she ever see him like this again? Her throat closed as she realised the answer was probably no.

The bed sank as he sat, facing her. Luisa's heart squeezed.

'You're pregnant.' It was a statement.

'I think so. But if I am it's your child.' She met his impenetrable gaze defiantly. 'It's got nothing to do with Lukas.'

He reached out and smoothed a lock of hair off her brow. Luisa's breath caught at the seeming tenderness of the gesture. She told herself she was a fool.

'I didn't think it had.'

'Oh.' She sank back, stunned.

'Have you seen a doctor?'

'No. It's still early.' She knew exactly when their baby had been conceived: that first tempestuous night of marriage, when she'd learned about ecstasy and heartache.

But Raul's calm acceptance surprised her. 'So you never thought—?'

He shook his head. 'I can't lie and say it didn't occur to me.' His eyes slid from hers. 'But when would you have time for an affair? It's *my* bed you share? *My* sofa. *My* desk.'

'You've made your point!' He didn't have to remind her how needy she was for him. How he only had to tilt one dark eyebrow in delicious invitation for her pulse to thrum with anticipation.

She stared hard into his face, trying to decipher his thoughts. Bewildered, she shook her head. 'I thought you'd believe—'

'That my wife was having an affair with my secretary?' Raul grimaced and placed has hand over hers. She felt heat, power and solidity, and she couldn't bring herself to dislodge his hand.

'I admit it was an unpleasant shock.' He tightened his hold and drew a deep breath that expanded his chest mightily. 'But I've come to know you, Luisa. You'd never go behind my back with another man. You're honest, genuine and caring. You wouldn't behave like that.' The words fell like nourishing rain in her parched soul.

He believed in her?

Her hands trembled with the shock of it.

'I know Lukas too,' he continued. 'We've worked together for years. How could I believe the worst, knowing you both?'

'I—' Words failed her. Such trust, when Raul had been so badly hurt before, and in the face of such evidence, stunned her. She'd expected a myriad of questions at the very least. Her heart swelled.

'I thought after Ana—'

'Forget Ana. I was a fool ever believing myself

in love with her. But I got over her years ago. This is about you and me, Luisa. No one else.'

Raul's intense stare pinioned her, even as relief flared deep inside at the knowledge the other woman was no rival for Raul's affection. She'd worried about that so long! A burgeoning sense of lightness filled her.

'Luisa.' Her name was a sudden hoarse rasp that startled her. 'I want you to stay. Here, with me. Don't go to Sydney.'

The trembling in her hands intensified as tenuous joy rose. He believed in her! He wanted her!

It took a moment to realise why.

Disillusionment was bitter on her tongue. She tried to pull away but his grasp tightened.

'Because of the baby! You want your heir.' That was why he'd changed his mind about her going. This was about bloodlines. How could she have thought otherwise? She knew to her cost how important royal blood was in this place. Her heart spasmed in distress.

'Of course I want to be with the baby and you.'

She shook her head, a lead weight settling on her chest. The pain was worse now, more intense after that single moment of hope. She almost cried out.

Despite her efforts to make a place for herself here, Luisa knew she was too impulsive, too casual, too ready to bend the rules to make a good monarch's wife.

It wasn't Luisa he wanted, just her unborn child.

'Please let go of me. This won't work.' She didn't know how she summoned the strength to speak calmly, when inside it felt as if she were crumbling.

For what seemed an age he held her, his gaze sharp on her face. Then finally, when she'd almost given up on him responding, he released her and turned away, his shoulders hunching.

Instantly Luisa missed his warmth, his strength. She looked at her hands, where he'd gripped her so tightly, and it hit her she wasn't trembling any more.

Stunned, she looked to Raul, the distracted way he shoved a hand through his hair. She stared, not believing what she saw.

It was *him*. He was shaking all over.

'Raul?' Luisa's voice sounded hollow, as if it came from far away. She didn't understand what was going on. Her big, strong husband shook like a leaf.

'Raul! What is it?'

He didn't answer and she reached out a tentative hand to his shoulder. She felt the tremors running through his large frame.

'Raul!' Fear welled. Was he ill?

'I can't. I...' His head sank between his shoulders.

Frantically Luisa tugged at his upper arm, turning him towards her. She rose onto her knees and shuffled closer.

'What is it? Please, tell me.'

Finally he swung his head towards her. He was haggard as she'd never seen him, his flesh drawn too tight across the bones. Only his eyes looked alive in that spare face. They glittered, overbright.

'I can't lose you, Luisa.' His voice was a whisper of anguish that tore at her. 'God help me, I can't let you go. When you said you had to get away I knew I couldn't force you to stay any longer. But...'

'Raul?' She gulped. 'I don't understand. What are you saying?'

Luisa stared, dumbfounded, at the man she'd heard give speeches in four languages, charming, persuasive Raul, struggling to get his words out. Her grip eased on his arm and her hand slid up in a soothing caress.

'I need to look after you, Luisa. You and our baby.' Her heart somersaulted at the sound of those words: *our baby.*

'We'll come to some arrangement.' Much as the idea of part-time parents pained her, she knew their baby needed them both.

'I don't want *an arrangement.*' He lifted his head, the glitter in his eyes different, almost dangerous. 'I want my wife and child. Here.' He reached out to grab a rolled up paper from the foot of the bed. 'This will prove how much I want you here.'

With fumbling hands he thrust it at her, almost ripping the thick parchment as he hastened to unroll it.

'It's all in Maritzian.' Despairingly she skimmed the document, too distracted to concentrate properly. All she took in was the column of seals and signatures at the bottom, beginning with the flourish of Raul's formal signature and the royal dragon seal.

'What is it, Raul?' She'd never seen him like this, so agitated she wanted to cradle him close.

'It authorises a change in the royal succession from the moment I'm crowned. On that day you'll become Queen.'

She frowned. 'That's no change.'

He shook his head. 'Queen, not royal consort. You'll be my equal, my partner in ruling the kingdom.' His gleaming gaze met hers and the force of it warmed her very soul. 'How else can I prove what you mean to me? How much I need and trust you?'

Her eyes widened. 'But you can't do that! I'm

not…not…I don't have the experience. I wouldn't know what to do. I—'

He grabbed her hands and held them tight. 'You'll learn. I'll teach you.' He kissed her palm and shivers of delight ran through her.

'But Maritz isn't ready for this. I'm not good at—'

'Maritz will adapt. You're capable and honest and caring. You'll make a perfect queen. For my country. For me. For our child.' His gaze dipped to her belly and heat sizzled through her.

'But I break all the rules.'

'Sometimes they need to be broken. There's more to life than protocol, you know.' He smiled, a slow, devastating smile that heated her from the soles of her feet to the top of her head.

'You're a princess to make anyone proud. Already our people respect and care for you, because they see how you care about them. You've helped them when it counted. You've helped *me*. You've changed my life and taught me hope.'

Luisa's brain whirled. It was too much to comprehend.

'Can you forgive me, Luisa? Enough to stay and give me another chance?'

She watched him swallow hard and searched her heart for a response. She loved him but was that enough to face the future? To build a life together even in the light of this momentous gesture of faith?

If he hauled her into his arms and swept her away on a tide of passion it would be easy to say yes. She yearned for that. But life wasn't so simple.

'It's not about forgiving the past. It's about the future.' She drew a difficult breath, wondering if he'd understand. 'I want a real marriage. A happy family. I want my child to enjoy being a child, with parents who really care. I want—'

'Love,' he finished for her on a husky whisper that pierced her. 'And trust and respect.' He nodded. 'You deserve it, Luisa. That's what I want to give you. If you'll let me try.'

Her breath caught in her throat at the look in his eyes.

'I love you, Luisa. I want you by my side.'

Dazed, Luisa stared into his tense face. A pulse jerked at the base of his neck and another beat at his temple. He looked like a man on the edge.

'It can't be,' she whispered, stunned into immobility.

'It's true.'

Silently she shook her head, afraid to believe.

'I didn't realise it myself.' His mouth twisted in a lopsided grimace that made her want to cuddle him close. 'I'd spent so long explaining away my feelings because the alternative was too terrifying. All my adult life I've worked to shut off my emotions. Then you came along. You made me *feel* so much, so intensely.'

Raul threaded his fingers through hers and tingling heat spread through her bloodstream. 'I've been torn, regretting the way I forced you here, forced you to marry me.' His eyes flashed. 'Yet knowing that in my heart I couldn't be truly sorry because it brought you to me and I couldn't let you go. How selfish is that?'

He thrust his other hand through his glossy hair in a distracted gesture that made her want to wrap her arms around him. 'I'd told myself for so long that love was a fool's game. And here I was falling for a woman who had every reason to hate me.'

'I don't hate you.' The admission slipped out. She was numb, dazed.

'Really?' Hope blazed in his eyes. 'Then it's far more than I deserve.' His hand moved up to stroke her cheek and thread into her hair. Hope whispered through her.

'I've been torturing myself, telling myself I should find the strength to let you walk away and be happy.' His hold tightened.

He brought their joined hands up so he could kiss her wrist. 'But I can't do it. I have to fight for you.'

'Tell me again,' she whispered, her voice uneven. 'Tell me you love me.'

Raul lifted both hands, tenderly bracketing her face.

'I love you, Luisa. Never doubt it. I want to be by your side always. To share with you, be the one you turn to. Teach you to waltz and whatever else you want if you'll share your warmth and your laughter with me.'

Something shifted deep inside her. A tightness eased and Luisa drew breath, it seemed for the first time in an age.

'Oh, Raul!' She choked with emotion. 'I've loved you so long. I never thought…' She blinked furiously as tears welled.

'Truly?' His voice was husky with awe.

She nodded and gentle fingers wiped the wetness from her cheeks. 'Truly. Desperately.'

'My darling!' His forest-dark eyes meshed with hers. 'I didn't mean to make you cry, sweetheart. I only want to make you happy. Always.'

'You do.' She blinked and smiled. 'I've been happy here with you.'

She saw doubt and fear etched across his features. Uncertainty in the man who'd strode into her life and grabbed her destiny in his strong hands. Who ruled a kingdom with an ease anyone would envy.

'I'll make mistakes,' he admitted. 'This is all new to me. I've never felt like this.' He swallowed hard and she read a flicker of anxiety in his eyes. 'I'm not a good risk, I know. I don't have your gift of closeness and warmth. I have no experience of real family life. No role model of how to be a good father—'

Luisa's fingers on his lips stopped his words. Her heart contracted, seeing the man she loved unsure of himself.

Seeing his self-doubt, Luisa knew the truth. She had to cast off her own fear. She had to trust, in him and in herself and put the past behind her.

'I'm willing to try if you are,' she whispered in a voice croaky with emotion. It welled inside, making her whole being tremble.

Dark eyes met hers and the love she read there made her poor bruised heart squeeze tight.

'Luisa!' He gathered her close, kissing her neck, her cheeks. He held her as if she was the most precious thing in the world.

It was glorious, but it wasn't enough. Not when her heart soared with wonderment.

She cupped his hard jaw and pressed her lips full on his mouth. Instantly he responded, his mouth hungry, as if it had been a lifetime since they'd kissed. As if they'd never kissed.

Not really.

Not like this.

Raul's kiss healed. It was demanding, possessive, yet poignantly sweet. A giving and receiving, not just of physical delight but of love. True love.

Eventually they pulled apart, enough to gulp in much needed air. But Raul's arms were locked close around her and Luisa's hands were clamped tight at his shoulders.

Happiness surged so strongly she felt incandescent with it.

'I can't believe this is real.'

His shining eyes met hers and her heart somersaulted when she read the tenderness there. 'Let me show you how real, my sweet.' He gathered her close and kissed her till the world fell away.

EPILOGUE

THE ballroom was packed. Out in the courtyard more people gathered beneath fluttering royal banners, garlands and gilded lanterns.

Cheers reverberated off the antique mirrors and frescoed ceiling as the crowd applauded their new rulers: King Raul and Queen Luisa. The first joint monarchs in Maritzian history.

Goosebumps rose on Luisa's bare arms as she heard their names shouted once, twice, three times, first by the herald and then by the swelling voices of the throng.

On her head sat a delicate diadem of pure gold and dazzling brilliant cut diamonds. In her hand rested the mediaeval bejewelled orb and in Raul's, seated beside her, the engraved golden sceptre.

She breathed deep, hardly daring to believe this moment was real. But then a warm hand enfolded hers and squeezed. She turned and fell into the warm green depths of Raul's loving gaze.

It was real. The ceremony, the crowd, but most important of all, Raul's love.

He raised her hand and pressed a fervent kiss there. Instantly excitement shot through her. And anticipation.

He smiled, a devilish light in his eyes and she knew her expression gave her away. He read her feelings for him on her face. She didn't care. She revelled in their love.

And this was only the beginning…

Raul laughed and through the haze of well-being she heard the crowd applaud again.

She turned and looked down from her throne. There was Lukas standing with Luisa's new secretary, Sasha. From this angle it looked like they held hands. Then there were Tamsin and Alaric, their smiles conspiratorial. Mary and Sam were in the front row, in places of honour, beaming at Luisa as if it were the most natural thing that she should marry a king and rule a country.

She shook her head in wonderment.

'Are you ready, sweetheart?'

Raul rose and drew her to her feet. Officials appeared to take the precious orb and sceptre.

'Ready as I'll ever be.' He led her down from the dais to the polished floor where space was made for them.

'You'll be fine,' he murmured and pulled her into

his arms. 'If there's a problem, blame it on your teacher.'

She gazed into his eyes, ablaze with love, felt him swing her into a waltz and smiled. The music soared and she whirled in the arms of the man she adored. She was home.

* * * * *